FOUND AUDIO

A NOVEL BY
N.J. CAMPBELL

Two Dollar Radio
Books too loud to ignore

Two Dollar Radio
Books too loud to Ignore

WHO WE ARE TWO DOLLAR RADIO is a family-run outfit dedicated to reaffirming the cultural and artistic spirit of the publishing industry. We aim to do this by presenting bold works of literary merit, each book, individually and collectively, providing a sonic progression that we believe to be too loud to ignore.

TWODOLLARRADIO.com

Proudly based in
Columbus
OHIO

🐦 @TwoDollarRadio

📷 @TwoDollarRadio

f /TwoDollarRadio

Love the
PLANET?
So do we.

Printed on Rolland Enviro, which contains 100% post-consumer fiber, is ECOLOGO, Processed Chlorine Free, Ancient Forest Friendly and FSC® certified and is manufactured using renewable biogas energy.

PERMANENT   100%   BIO GAS ENERGY   Ancient Forest Friendly™

Printed in Canada

SOME RECOMMENDED LOCATIONS FOR READING *FOUND AUDIO*: Base Camp on Mount Everest; In the eye of a tropical hurricane; On the shores of infinity; In the glow of a dying campfire with dawn on the horizon; Motocross rallies; Antarctica; The Horsehead Nebula; Labyrinthine libraries; Pretty much anywhere because books are portable and the perfect technology!

AUTHOR PHOTOGRAPH →
Hannah Foster

COVER DESIGN →
Two Dollar Radio

Thank you for supporting independent culture!
Feel good about yourself.

FOUND
AUDIO

Foreword

In 2006, I received the following manuscript and was asked to find a publisher for it. I have taken that request, in turns, as both a challenge and a crusade. In the fall of 2016, I finally succeeded.

As it stands, only one section forms a semi-coherent whole. That section is a detailed description of what appears to be three consecutive audio interviews. The following documents which include the transcriber's letter to my former employer and her note on the text are here included for background and context on the interviews themselves.

As much as possible, these documents are here duplicated without revision, censorship, or alteration. The only substantial additions are the section headers inserted to make clear what was intended as the original manuscript and what has been added for context. Beyond these additions, only spelling errors have been corrected in the text for clarity and ease of reading.

For reasons of permission and privacy, some names have been redacted at the request of the publisher.

N.J. Campbell
Fairfield, Iowa
March 19, 2017

Transcriber's Letter

Office of Amrapali Anna Singh, PhD.
University of Dutch Harbor
14–B South Nunavut Street
Dutch Harbor, AK 99692

April 8, 2006

Dear ██████████,

   The strange circumstances that have brought me to write this letter are not few in number, but I would like to apologize in advance if I'm taking any liberties in sending you a rough, unfinished first draft of a non-fiction work in progress.

   I'm sure you don't remember, but we met once at the conference 'Sound in Written Texts' in Phoenix in the fall of 2004. I was there giving a lecture on my book, *What We've Lost With Digital: The Drawbacks of Compression in New Audio Media,* and you said you enjoyed my talk. I was flattered, and joked that I would naturally love to have my work published with one of the reputable presses you work for. You were encouraging with your response, suggesting I send you something if I ever had a manuscript that was more narrative-driven or exciting. The good news is that I believe this is exciting. The bad news is that it's so exciting I had to send it very quickly, for reasons which I will explain in my note on the text.

Sincerely,
A.A. Singh
*Professor, Archival Studies; Linguistics; Modern and Classical Languages
School of Humanities*

Transcriber's Note on the Text

On March 23, 2006, I received a visit in my office in Dutch Harbor, Alaska, from a Mr. Pierre Cavey. Mr. Cavey had come a great distance to see me because of my specialized skill set.

To explain, I am a research historian who received her doctorate in archival studies with a specialization in the authentication and examination of antiquated audio formats. In layman's terms, I determine the authenticity of source materials and other specialized information in audio formats from earlier periods. I have worked with everything from CDs to phonographs, and I did my dissertation on the techniques necessary to determine whether or not an audio sample had been transferred from a long-playing record to an 8-track tape. I have since discovered and refined the only procedures available on how to determine the possible time of day and temperature of a room during the recording of a non-digital audio format. I have worked with the governments of Japan, Malaysia, and Russia on archival restoration projects, and I have written three books: *The Sound of Temperature*, *The Sound of Time*, and a historical study of analog recording methods, *What We've Lost With Digital: The Drawbacks of Compression in New Audio Media*.

I would never consider myself to be a particularly interesting or noteworthy person. The most exciting thing I have to do on a given day is decide which headphones I'm going to use. My work is often dull and always arduous, so when Mr. Cavey stepped into my office on the afternoon of Monday, March 20, with the eyes of an adoring fan, I was a little less than convinced of his enthusiasm and a little more than annoyed at his interruption. At the time, I was working very hard on monitoring a subtle aspect of sound translation between formats with discrete increments of transistor amplification to be included in a new publication. Although he could see that I was in a moment of extreme focus, he started talking loudly enough to drown out any of the noise coming through my headphones.

He said that he had come directly from Buenos Aires by way of Shanghai, Allahabad, and Antananarivo with three Type IV audio cassettes, and that he was very excited to work with me on finding out anything I could tell him about them. I told him frankly that an e-mail would have been sufficient for our correspondence, and that I wasn't really interested in amateur audio analysis. He said that this was not an amateur endeavor and that Claude D. Montclair, PhD., professor of the History of Audio Design at the University of Northwestern Paris, had recommended my work. At that point, I was very upset, as Claude had said he was sending me something interesting, but he didn't say he was sending anyone with it. I enjoy my work, but I don't really enjoy working with people. If I enjoyed working with people, I would have gone into audio engineering. But I digress, and, really, my lack of focus is only due to the contents of the transcription you are about to read and the correspondence surrounding it. As I re-read what I have just written in the last paragraph, the sequencing of my thoughts is reasonable, though I must also apologize. For if I had more time, I would be able to give these few pieces of attendant information a second pass for editing and correction. In the future, I hope to produce a more refined edit of these documents, but as I wanted to get these items in the mail as soon as possible, I cannot spend any more time on them at present. And now that I think of it, the letter of introduction above will probably seem like the most well-thought-out document in this proposal. To be honest, I waited to prepare this note last, knowing it was the most important to the text, but not knowing I'd need to prepare it so quickly. You see, I thought I had several weeks, months, or even years before approaching you. Alas, given the circumstances, I must send it out today with the mail, and the pickup here in Dutch Harbor is less than two hours away.

Now, to get back to my introduction to Mr. Cavey and his tapes. To give you a better idea of the man, I need to say that aside from his general excitement, he was a tall, thin, and well-groomed gentleman who wore a black tie and a black suit on both of the occasions of our association. Whether that was his only suit, his traveling suit, just one of his suits, or a uniform, I can't say, but I can say the clothes fit his frame perfectly. Beyond that, he self-identified as an 'archive archeologist of sorts.' The term was completely ridiculous to me, as one is either an archivist or an archeologist. If—and I have no reason to believe any such thing actually exists—such a thing does exist, its field of scope would be miniscule, as recorded history is limited and reasonably well-documented by several subsets of archivist already. Nevertheless, had I not found him and the objects in his possession interesting, I would not be sitting here writing about them in any great detail.

But, onto the objects themselves. The tapes in his possession, he told me, were of personal importance and of potentially remarkable consequence. In my life, I have seen less than a dozen items of such a proposed consequence, though I have been told everything from someone's personal collection of Barry Manilow LPs to a cassette tape of Nelson Mandela talking in his sleep during his time in prison was of vital significance, and that if I could just help the enthusiastic hobbyist confirm the details of X, Y, and Z with my equipment and expertise, I was sure to come into not only great industry acclaim, but untold popular adoration as well. Ridiculous, absolutely ridiculous in almost every case. Although, I will say that once I was able to confirm that an undocumented recording of Erik Satie was actually the man himself, though that's the type of thing that one in my position dreams about, not something one is likely to see. Even so, the items in his possession sounded—by definition—technically unique, in that he said the take-up reel, supply reel, and guide rollers were in near flawless condition for their age and for the amount of use he assured me they had endured. I was, of course, still very skeptical, as there were obvious signs of aging on the items before me. The casing was not mint by any account and the tape itself had obviously been played numerous times—but that those heavily used parts showed no visible signs of wear indicated to me that they had either been replaced or were truly of a remarkable quality and design. Upon inspection, I discovered that the tape had not been re-attached, nor had it been doctored in any way. I also found that the metal used for the tension arms and scrape filters was 24k gold. Still, even all of that taken together was not anything to write home about. Life is full of bizarre coincidence. That life exists at all is an exceptionally bizarre coincidence. But my objections to the items' 'remarkable consequence' notwithstanding, he went on at length to explain that the contents were, in actuality, so fascinating and so interesting and so fantastic that I would come to believe it was a privilege just to inspect them. Can you imagine that kind of hubris? I can't stand it when people say they have the 'prettiest pony' I've never seen. It's almost certainly never a unicorn. I didn't even touch the fact that I had examined analog audio recordings not only from Erik Satie, but also Gandhi, Amelia Earhart, and Albert Einstein, not to mention more than a dozen other individuals of great consequence. So, at this point, I was visibly upset and telling him that if he didn't want to vacate my office, I was happy to ask security to help him do so. It was then that he threw up his hands and said he could pay. To be clear, I don't mean that he was willing to throw me $50 for my trouble, but that he was prepared to offer me $20,000 in cash for one, possibly two days of work. I, being well aware of the financial limitations of a primarily academic lifestyle, said yes, as long as he paid up front. Much to my surprise, he produced four envelopes, each holding $5,000. It was Monday afternoon and, all of a sudden, I had $20,000 on my desk. Of course, my first thought was that he might be involved in some illegal activity, but as he was involved with Claude, a man with whom I had worked closely on several occasions and who was adamant about obeying every form of copyright and traffic law of every country I had ever worked with him in, not to mention his strict adherence to international style guides for scholarly attribution, I knew the man standing before me was almost certainly not of nefarious origin. I also knew how far that amount of money would go toward certain select pieces of audio equipment that I could put to good use in my studio at home. So, for better or for worse—and for all that is interesting in this manuscript— I took the money and said I'd do what I could for him, depending on the information he required. He said that he wanted to know everything I could determine about where the recordings were made, in what conditions they were produced, when they were recorded, and, if possible, who might have recorded them. I asked if he wanted any duplicates made, and he said that going forward our arrangement was based on the understanding that I was in no way to reproduce the contents of the tapes. I then told him I would be able to give him a more detailed work-up if given more than two days' time, but he refused and said it wouldn't be possible as he was taking the tapes to Minsk at that point. I then explained that given his extremely limited time-frame, I'd do the best I could, but that I probably wouldn't be able to perform any miracles. After that, I informed him he could pick up the materials on Wednesday when whatever analysis I could finish would be done. He thanked me and left.

Of course, all of that was fine with me, as I felt a bit like a bandit making off with a large sum of stolen money. I had duly informed the man that the scope and content of my analysis would most likely be shallow with his time constraints, and I didn't even have to factor in time and materials to make him any copies! It was a dream come true. The only drawback was that I really wasn't looking forward to the material. The analysis, I assumed, would be the equivalent of listening to paint dry. And, much to my surprise, I was wrong. From the moment

Mr. Cavey left the room, I started to smell something on the tapes. When I first played them, I realized that the smell was really two smells—the smell of old books and what I think is incense. I am familiar with the smell of old books, but I am almost completely unfamiliar with any of the smells associated with incense. This was charming, but otherwise un-noteworthy. I don't have much time before the post office closes, yet I feel the need to include as many specific details as possible, for clarity's sake, and because explication is the better part of my job and nature. I apologize, again, for the rambling tone, although without any extra time, it seems regrettably unavoidable to me.

Now, the tapes themselves were standard matte black and were banded together simply with a rubber band. On the front of each tape was an individual designation, 779J.2314.PPJQ, 779J.2314.PPJR, and 779J.2314.PPJS, and on the back there was the name and address of their library of origin:

Biblioteca Nacional de Investigación de Buenos Aires
Colecciones especiales, la habitación #347
Avenida Independencia 7765–12B
Capital Federal 1431
Argentina

Attribution was obvious. Mr. Cavey didn't need me for that, though oftentimes libraries cannot provide the type of detailed information that I can with respect to the audio sample itself, so rather than assume that the man had missed this conspicuous detail, I assumed that he already knew everything he needed to about it. I did, however, look up the address on the internet and found that the library in question had recently moved and that all future inquiries were to be forwarded to a new address in care of the postmaster. I made a note of the new information and began to pay more careful attention to what I could discover about the tapes.

Initially, I wasn't really interested in the amateur fictional accounts I was listening to. Fiction, of course, is what I thought I was hearing. The elements of the stories on each of the tapes were, to my taste, cliché, undeveloped, and hackneyed, but, then again, I only really enjoy reading Shakespeare or, sometimes, Proust, in my free time, so I'm not generally a good judge of the merit of contemporary imaginative prose. That said, there was an element to it—something I found both vulgar and seductive, like the sound of ambulance sirens in the distance. I listened to their content once, and then I ran them through some of my equipment and subsequent analysis. After the first day, I had concluded that the rough temperature readings—that is, sound variance based on humidity present at the time of recording—within each of the tapes were wildly variable, and that the indications of location I could pick up on in each tape's background noise differed to an impossible degree. I picked up, within one tape, noises from the streets of either Chicago or Detroit, the jungles of Northern Thailand, and wind patterns most familiar to the Antarctic, as well as a noise I had only ever encountered once before. It was a particularly difficult sound, something I hadn't been able to isolate on a recording I had transcribed of Gandhi's from a 1924 speech on non-violence. Registering like a cross between a snake's hiss and a B-52's engine, it remained both distinct and blended at the same time, almost as if it were two sets of sounds, each playing feedback to one another and each almost cancelling the other out. Of course I would have concluded that someone was putting me on, except you can't fake those sounds on analog formats. You can play a recording in a room in order to record it onto another recording, but that creates a shadow that's relatively obvious to my ear, let alone my equipment. So, I double-checked my measurements, and then I listened to each of the recordings again. I then deliberated as to whether or not I should copy the tapes, even though it went against the explicit wishes of my employer. Of course, initially, I had no intentions of doing so, as I consider myself an honest person with professional standards, but after listening to each tape several more times through, I became curious about a few other aspects as well. I wondered if some of the tapes' inconsistencies might be able to serve certain capacities in some of my other on-going research projects, and, eventually, I came to consider one or two qualities of each tape unique, like the one I just described. As such, I was faced with the problem of knowing they were potentially invaluable in terms of their research application. For a while, I questioned whether or not it was my ear, false readings from my equipment, or actual facets of the tapes themselves. About that point, I also started to see the material being discussed on the tapes as vaguely compelling, and I knew that I was without perspective. Perhaps the tapes had scientific value, perhaps the broader public needed to be made aware of whatever was happening on them, but whatever the case, I knew I couldn't be certain of exactly what was going on without further investigation and peer review. So, in an attempt to avoid a potentially irreplaceable loss or grievous error, I took a personal risk and decided to spend the rest of my time creating a detailed transcription of the tapes and my notes, as well as making copies of the tapes themselves. By the time I had finished my task, I had become clear in my conviction that they do hold value—to one degree or another—and that it is only a matter of determining that degree before making sure the material reaches a broader audience.

When Mr. Cavey returned, he was smiling. I said that I had much more to offer him than I thought I would, and he said he knew a person of my facility and expertise wouldn't be able to resist them. I told him what I've just explained to you, and I also gave him a copy of my technical readouts. Unfortunately, as the readouts are copious and I have only the one other copy right now with no time to make another, I am sending those materials to a colleague, Marilyn Eldritch of the University of Chicago, who is also capable of analyzing the data rigorously, corroborating my findings, and holding the materials till I am able to go over them with her at a later date over the phone or over e-mail correspondence while I travel.

I did ask Mr. Cavey if he could tell me anything about the library in Buenos Aires, and he told me that wouldn't be possible. I asked if he was sure he wouldn't like me to make a transcription of the tapes, and he said that wouldn't be necessary. I asked him if I could have his e-mail, phone number, or address for further correspondence on the items, and he said that he wasn't interested in giving any of them to me. I gave up, handed him the tapes and the readouts, and accompanied him out of the building. I have not seen or heard from him since. The named journalists in the tapes, Julien Belmonte and Bianca Terrazas, as far as I can tell, have never published or been mentioned in anything I can find anywhere on the internet. Their names seem to be vacuums without digital footprints. Again, this lends itself to the following account being fiction—making this whole thing an elaborate charade. However, I am convinced that it is not, and that the events described within this document are not only real, but also something more than real can be. And, as my copies may be confiscated from me at some point, and with them my ability to do further research, I thought it best to leave my only spare copy of the transcription in your capable hands. I mention that they may be confiscated not because I am afraid that someone will take them, but because things can become lost and files can become deleted. It's also important now to mention my reason for rushing these documents to you: I wrote the library in Buenos Aires, as they have no listed e-mail address, for any information regarding the recordings or any other recordings containing content of a similarly abstract nature. And as source materials are valuable objects, I assumed they might have chosen to invite me to see the collection for myself or inform me of the impossibility of such an occasion. Instead they wrote me the reply which I have photocopied and included below:

***

BIBLIOTECA NACIONAL DE INVESTIGACIÓN DE BUENOS AIRES
COLECCIONES ESPECIALES,
LA HABITACIÓN #347 — RECUPERACIÓN

***

March 29, 2006

Dear Amrapali Anna Singh, PhD.,

We are interested in information leading to the reclamation of the stolen property you made mention
of in your recent correspondence. A Reclamation
Agent is en route to you as you read this note, and we
would be very grateful for any help you could give
us that might lead to the detention of Pierre Cavey.

As for your request to have further pieces of the collection sent to you, that will not be possible. As for
visiting our premises, that may be possible. You will
find out in more detail when our Reclamation Agent
reaches you on April 10, 2006.

In Expectation,
Room #347

INTERNO REFERENCIA: RR-UO-X3179-Beta.37

In addition to this letter, I've also received calls about Mr. Cavey from the U.S. Embassy in Argentina and the Argentinean Embassy in D.C., both mentioning the severity of Mr. Cavey's crimes and the potential necessity of my needing to give a deposition against him in person. Now you are aware of the reasons I have decided to send these things out hastily. If I am to be traveling, then I want to know that I have copies other than the ones in my own possession available to be sent to me, as I am hoping to go over them in detail with one of the library's representatives in Buenos Aires. You may also be wondering why I haven't just sent all the materials to my colleague in Chicago. To be frank, I want to see her transcript of the materials and her notes without the help of my own. This, of course, will create a stronger corroboration, and, in turn, will only benefit the manuscript itself. Also, I wanted to declare my intention to publish this material, in case my colleague is as eager to do so as I am. I know I would be eager if the situation were reversed. And as for my travels, who knows? Maybe I'll return with even more interesting information, in which case I will forward my findings to you accordingly.

Finally, I must apologize for the rough formatting of the transcribed material. I have done the best I could with the time I've had, but as it stands, there are still several notes in the margin of the text with regards to aspects of the recordings I've second-guessed myself on. Also, it's important to note that I've tried to identify whose voice was speaking, in what language, and with what, if any, accent, but this definitely needs further review. I've marked such notation in brackets. At present, I'm about 80 percent sure of the attributions I've made, but there are curious irregularities in the raw audio data itself, though I have no time to go into detail about that now.

Sincerely,
A.A. Singh

The Tapes

779J.2314.PPJQ
[Tape I]

Date recorded: <u>Approx. 1998</u>
<u>Pure CrO2 coating</u>
<u>AC bias 79.8-82.1 kHz</u>
mostly minimal hysteresis / some variable hysteresis

[Male, Age: 48–52, United States American, Midwestern Accent. Designation: "American"]

[American]: In '91 I went down to the bayou, because I had heard of a man who bounty-hunted snakes—not water moccasins or any other native snake, but pythons and anacondas and big-game species that had been imported as house pets from Southeast Asia and dumped into the bayou. They bred and became invasive species. Actually, now there's a hunting season for invasive snake species in the South every year in the Everglades with prize money for the largest haul. The name of the man I was looking for was Otha Johnson. He was a Louisiana native that I had heard of when doing a piece for *National Geographic* on the shifting waterways of the Everglades. A friend, the French-Algerian journalist Julien Belmonte, had mentioned him in passing as one of the 'natural wonders' in the area. He said that as this man's full-time occupation was to hunt and kill snakes for the Department of Natural Resources, he was sure to be a good story. He said that he had actually tried to track him down a few years before, while he was working with my ex—the award-winning journalist Bianca Terrazas—on an assignment about modern-day trappers. I thought, if they couldn't do it, I wanted to, and I immediately started doing some background research on the guy.

I called around the National Park Service, the Federal Bureau of Land Management, the Fish and Wildlife Service, the USDA's Natural Resource Conservation Office—hell, I even called the EPA, asking for information on any special projects they had to employ such a person, as it seemed so incredible, but no one could tell me anything. I assumed it was bureaucratic incompetence and started calling the local authorities. I called two or three different offices before I got a man by the name of Dale... Dale something or other. I can't think of the rest of his name off the top of my head, but I'm sure it was in my notes at the time. At any rate, when I mentioned Otha's name, the other end of the line went silent. I waited a moment, and then I asked if he knew the man.

'Yeah, I know Otha Johnson,' Dale said in a very particular way that I can't easily describe. There was a mixture of certainty and hesitation in his voice... I know that's not a very good description, but it's the only way I can think to describe it.

I asked if he knew who his employer was.

Dale laughed what sounded like a tight-lipped laugh and said, 'That's a matter of opinion.'

I said that I was under the impression that he was paid by the United States government or, maybe, the state of Louisiana, to hunt species of invasive snakes.

'Maybe so, I'm not very sure of that,' he said.

Then I asked if I was in fact calling the Louisiana Department of Wildlife, Fisheries, and Parks—just to make sure I had the right number.

He affirmed that was the agency I had called and added, 'Otha Johnson goes by many names. I'm not sure what his legal name is, so I couldn't tell you if he's a federal or state contractor... What business did you say you have with Otha, again?'

I said that I was interested in doing a piece on him for a wildlife magazine.

Dale chuckled and said, 'He is wildlife.'

I asked what exactly he meant by that, as I was trying to learn as much as I possibly could from one of the only people I had talked to that knew who I was referring to.

He said something like, 'Otha is a strange thing. He's been around longer than our offices have been in existence. Before that, the sheriff was aware of him. Before that, I only know what the sheriff knew.'

'Would you mind telling me about what you do know about his affiliation with the parks department—or any other government office?' I asked, determined to get something more.

'As I'm not referring to a man by his legal name, let alone any Christian name—only an alias at best—I don't at all,' Dale started, and then went on to talk about how he knew Otha was born on the swamp, raised on the swamp, and hunted the swamp before the legality of who owned the land came into question in the late '50s when it was becoming protected land. You see, the problem was, Otha's family had been there a very long time, longer than the United States had been a country by Dale's understanding. He said that as the sheriff had described it to him, that the sheriff before that sheriff had told him that the Johnsons were African by way of French immigration in the 17th century.

Here, Dale acknowledged that this sounded more like myth and hearsay than fact, but that I had asked, and this is what he had been told by the sheriff back when the Department of Wildlife was being formed. Dale's department only had a concern with the Johnsons because the department had seized their land as public property without knowing that it had been occupied. When the land was being acquired for protection, of course, several commercial claims came forward, but none of them were of any legal consequence. However, a residential stake in the land holds greater weight in the courts, and when they found out someone had been living on the land they seized, they became nervous and started asking around about the Johnsons.

The way Dale understood it, in the end, the Department of Wildlife made an allowance for the Johnson family in perpetuity to live on the land with the stipulation that they make no large alterations to their allotment or hunt any of the wildlife in the area. Everyone agreed, and things were mostly fine, except, after a while, rumors began to surface that the Johnsons were selling hides and swamp meat to poachers.

The Department of Wildlife asked for the help of local law enforcement, and the sheriff's office said that it was a lost cause. That was the scandal—the Johnsons had been accused of hunting on private property across four counties, and never once had they been caught on another person's land or in possession of any contraband. The department thought this must have been due to local incompetence, and so they set out on their own to catch one of the Johnsons, but in 17 attempts, not a single carcass was found. Every time they asked one what they were doing, they said, 'Re-creational boatin',' after they had learned many years ago that that was the only acceptable answer.

I asked if it was possible that Otha had ended up being paid to do what they could never catch him doing, and Dale said many things were possible, but he had no knowledge of any such arrangement with him or any other person. He said that he did know there was an unofficial order to leave the person I knew as Otha Johnson alone, as any money spent on catching him was as good as money spent on catching unicorns.

At this point, I thought Otha sounded like the bayou version of Davy Crockett or Paul Bunyan—a hero of the swamp, fighting as an underdog against an oppressive system. He sounded like what he was—which was larger than life.

I tracked Otha down after piecing together leads Julien had handed off to me. There wasn't much to go on, and most of the people he and Bianca had talked to couldn't get straight which of the others had moved away or which had died. The community was mostly composed of retired tank-factory workers, and as that factory had gone under almost twenty years before, there wasn't much of a community left to speak of. Those that were still around paid lip service to having known trappers who had come and gone, but often enough couldn't remember what day of the week it was. At a dead end, I expanded my search to include those individuals who keep a running tally of personal histories, local lore, and hearsay in small communities across rural America—dry cleaners, bartenders, and barbers. I started with the barbers, and as I found only one in the phone book, it didn't take me long to track him down. Stan, the owner and only barber at Stan's Barber Shop, said he didn't know a tracker named Otha, but that I should stop by the VFW on Thursday night for the all-you-can-eat fried chicken and dumpling dinner, as that's where hunting and fishing stories were told in the area. I mentioned I wasn't a veteran, but he said it didn't matter. As it was the only bar in three counties, everybody went. So, I showed up the following Thursday, paid my $2.99 for the buffet, and asked around. The people there were friendly, but no one knew who I was talking about. Disappointed, but well fed, I stuck around to listen to stories of other trappers and the description of a generally wilder community of days past until a woman who looked to be around 60 came over to my stool at the bar. She was 5'2", had short gray hair, and couldn't have weighed more than a 120 pounds. She was wearing a denim jacket, gray canvas pants and black leather gloves, and she stank of gin. She introduced herself as Big Tilly and said she knew the man I was looking for. I asked if she might take me to him, but she said it didn't work like that. When I asked how it worked, she said it worked the way she said it did—I'd pay her for her services, and then I'd pay Otha for his, no questions asked. I could take it or leave it—that was it. I agreed, knowing full well she could be putting me on, but as she only asked me to pick up her bar tab, I figured her side of the bargain was the right price. Of course, she didn't tell me she had been drinking all day, every day for the last week, but I didn't figure that out till after she was gone. Once the deal had been struck, she wrote the name of a diner, a county road, and a time on a napkin and said he'd be there in two days. As the deal was no-questions-asked, I kept my mouth shut and kept drinking. Big Tilly ordered one last gin, drank it straight, and walked out the door. I paid her $88 tab consisting mostly of gin and egg salad sandwiches and showed up two days later at around 8 a.m. at Claire's Diner on Bukuru County route D-67.

I had some time between trips to Africa and China for several wilderness mags, and I wanted to see if I could write something I could sell on spec about this guy.[1]

Otha Johnson was, and is to this day, the most interesting man I've ever met, and I've not led a sheltered life: jungles of India, Sahara, Arctic, Everest, et cetera. But this guy was something completely different.

When I walked into the diner, he was the only one in the room. I don't mean that there weren't other people there, but this man's whole... presence, for lack of a better word, was magnetic, like something unreal. He had his eyes on me from the door. His face was blacker than coal and the whites of his eyes were bright ivory. He looked like one of those pulp magazine covers from *Weird Tales* about the jungles of Africa from the 1930s—strong and lean and youthful, though he wasn't quite a young man, maybe 55, 60. Anyway, I sat down and then he stopped looking at me. He looked out the window for what seemed like ages. I remember the window was fogged from the humidity. It was hot in the restaurant and it was hot outside, but the heat spread like melted butter over every glass surface. Finally, he spoke. Now, to be fair, I remember the feel of what I said and what he said, but not the exact words, so I'll do him as best as I can.

'What chu want from all dis sweat, all dis snake chasin'?' he said.

---

1 Here, concurrently with the narrator speaking for 22 seconds, I hear the sound of a propeller plane flying overhead. The distance is difficult to gauge.

I wanted a story I could sell to a popular magazine, some narrative about someone that people would be interested in but have no real way of relating to except as an oddity. You know, like people write things about today. Bullshit, plain and simple. You know it, I know it. The end. So I said, 'To tell your story, the story of a snake hunter in the bayou.'

And I remember this next part very clearly. He said: 'Nah, dat ain't it...' And then he paused again, and then he said, 'but we's go anyway.'

And I'm sitting there thinking, that was weird—did that guy just get inside my head, or did he pull a bluff, or can he read me like the front page of the *Sunday Times*? But then, I thought, he's probably just crazy. I mean, Julien, who first told me about him, said he heard he was a little odd, albeit he also heard he was an amazing tracker and hunter who could rival the best—and Julien had seen the best. When he was on assignment in Indonesia in the early '80s, he saw a two-man crew in a raft made completely out of empty plastic bottles take a single hand-carved butea-tree spear out into the ocean and then come back with a dead sperm whale in tow. And Dale, well, he obviously had his own lasting impressions of the man.

So, I'm sitting there, wondering all this and the guy gets up to leave. He walks out the door and I follow him. He gets in his truck. I get in his truck. He starts it and we drive away—in silence.

We drive a bit and it starts to get a little greener and grayer and we're heading deeper and deeper into the bayou. So I ask him if I can record some of his answers to my questions and he nods, so I start asking him questions.

'Where were you born? Where did you grow up? Where did you go to school? Where do you live?'

He just drives on, never looks at me, and says, 'Da bayou.'

I ask if he could be more specific. He uses his index finger and points out all around the view through the windshield.

All right, I think, this is going to be tough. So I pull what I think of as my wild card. Something that always works with people I've used it on in the past. I give him control over the conversation. I ask: 'What do you want to talk about?'

He just drives and stares.

Then he says, 'How much money you gonna pay me? Big Tilly says you pay me somethin' fo' my time.'

I say: 'Well, I don't know if there's a story here, so I don't know what I can pay.'

He slows the truck down, pulls over to the side of the road, and puts the truck transmission into park. The truck idles. I can hear it and the sound of the thickening swamp and that's it. I felt scared. I'm used to doing this, and feeling in control. That obviously wasn't what this was. So I say: 'Five hundred dollars.'

'No,' he says.

I say, 'One thousand dollars.'

He purses his lips and squints his eyes, and he says, 'All right, I got bills to pay, but yous gettin' da better end a dis deal.'

So we start moving, and I ask how old he is.

He says, 'Younger dan most a deese trees an' older dan some of 'em. Seasons roll much without change, but many some years. I guess by your mark nigh eighty.'

We drive on and the swamp makes it darker and darker, even though I know it's not even midday. Gray greens and mud browns darken everything and Otha looks like a shadow melting into the scenery. I've seen indigenous hunters deep in the Amazon look less naturally hidden than that man did inside his Ford Bronco in the backdrop of that foliage.

I think about asking questions, but I figure I can fill this part out with the mystery and intrigue of the man. Silence, if done well, can sell the right kind of piece.

And we go and go and it must have been hours, but you see, my watch had stopped sometime after leaving the hotel that morning, and I didn't know what time it was. I know, I know, this sounds made up, but I promise this is both stranger and less strange than it already seems. In that hot truck, as I only had my thoughts to keep me company, I thought about all the time it was taking us to get where we were going, and then I thought about all the time I had spent waiting in my life, and then I thought of Bianca. The circumstances reminded me of when she was working on a long piece that was eventually published in an anthology of different perspectives on sports journalism. You see, we had just gotten together—this must have been '83—and she decided to take on an interview with one of the most reclusive climbers in the world. A man who was said to be the best, but who wouldn't talk with anyone—went by the name of Andre. So—

[Female Inquirer, Age: 58–63, Sudanese/Australian accent with certain intonations indicating a third dialect, maybe Caribbean or Sioux Nation. Difficult to place. Designation: "Female, Tri-Accent"]

[Female, Tri-Accent]: Unacceptable. We require full names. Omissions will not be tolerated.

[Sound of metal on concrete. Sound of wooden board falling from a height of two to three feet.]

[American]: You didn't demand to know Dale's name. You didn't—

[Female, Tri-Accent]: 'Dale' is known. We are not concerned with 'Dale.' Who is 'Andre'?

[American]: Look—I've said Bianca's piece appeared in a book. You have her name in connection with this other individual. This isn't a test and I—

[Four seconds of the Larsen effect (feedback noise).]

[Female, Tri-Accent]: This is a test. This is all a test.

[…radio silence, dead audio of two minutes and 26 seconds with distinct indications of erasure followed by a site-credible one-second sound clip of tropical background noise and another site-credible one-second sound clip of temperate rainforest background noise, the second possibly including the call of a great horned owl...]

[American]: Yes, yes, I understand... ... ... Now... ... ... If I can continue... Will you? Yeah... So, the waiting reminded me of the time Bianca was away for those six months. We had basically just gotten together when she made a deal with Andre where he agreed to let her tag along with him and ask questions, if she agreed to do some climbing. Specifically, if she agreed to follow him up El Capitan at the end of the six months. Bianca had natural ability with almost anything she decided to do, and climbing was no different. By the end of the third month, she was a pretty decent amateur climber and driving me nuts. You see, I didn't mind that she was out with some other guy, climbing rocks in the middle of south-east Asia or the Australian outback, but I did mind that I couldn't even get a postcard to her. She would call me, occasionally, from a gas station pay phone and leave a message on my answering machine. I had no way to respond, and what she said always made me feel two things. One—that I'd never really be able to be with her, and two—that I'd never really be able to be without her. She'd say things like, 'I saw two baby joeys today and the sunset over Ayers rock. I love you.' Or, 'The wind came up from the south last night. I hope you're smiling when we summit Denali tomorrow.' It was like I was supposed to understand what she was saying, and I always felt like I almost did, but I could never understand it completely. I could never meet her the whole way. I guess it was just being near her that communicated the most, that made me... Anyway, about five months in, she left a message that said I could meet her at the top of El Capitan on July 7th. I remember the date because of what she said next. Now, I knew Andre fashioned himself as an unconventional climber—he was doing stuff in the early '80s that no one else was really doing until the late '90s, but I had no idea to what extent—no idea—until Bianca said they'd be free climbing the Bermuda Route on a moonless night while he experimented with a substance he called 'Blue.' That's when I got a little… a little uneasy. She did say that she wouldn't be taking any of this stuff, but that didn't matter. They were still going to be climbing in the dead of night with no harness, ropes, or safety gear of any kind. That was exactly the same type of waiting—expectant, nervous, and completely without any control—that reminded me of the waiting I was doing in that truck. I remember being there when she came up over the edge of that cliff at dawn. Her hands were covered in chalk and the look on her face was anything but easy to read, but it did, in a way, read me. I remember Andre looked neither happy nor sad, but completely at ease. The two of them just stood there in those separate but somehow similar states—right before the National Park police arrested them both on suspicion of drug trafficking. As they put the cuffs on her, she smiled at me and said, 'I understand.' And the next day, after I was able to bail her out, I said that I wanted to understand too. She looked at me and said, 'I know.' Then she went on to talk about what she had gotten out of her six months. A lot of it was just reverence for the natural world, which we both shared, but there was also a lot about Andre and his 'journey' as she said he called it. The way she talked about him was with a voice that was both sympathetic and uncertain—cautious and inspiring. She said that he climbed the way that he climbed—dosed on LSD or whatever else was around—because he was looking for 'the one place between night and day.' At least, that's what he called it. She explained that it wasn't dawn or twilight, but a state of being, a place that was neither becoming nor fading away. She said he thought he was close. He thought he was getting there—to that place that was neither coming nor going. Then she said that something about him made her understand something about me, something I wouldn't understand for a long time. Back then, I was just concerned with her safety. I was just glad she was all right and that the charges had been dropped against the both of them. And that's a lot of what I thought about driving down that long, narrow dirt road, sitting next to Otha Johnson.

But then we get to a shack rising from the mud beside a body of silty water that stretches into the distance. It's darker than it was earlier from the now total cover of the canopy, and Otha gets out of the truck. I follow him and as he opens the door to the shack, I'm hit with a strong sulfur smell. The hut is almost perfectly dark, except for a small fire against the back wall that seemed almost completely out, except that the flame was blue, which meant that it was a relatively hot fire. I stood outside waiting, and he moved around the inside quickly and quietly. I can recall thinking about the fire and how strong its smell was. I didn't wonder why he'd have a fire going in the middle of August in a Louisiana swamp—I'd seen other indigenous people do the same thing in parts of the Amazon and the Congo—it keeps things mostly dry and that's actually quite important when everything around you is, to some degree, wet. But the smell was so total, so complete, that I wondered how he could manage in there for more than a few minutes without suffocating, let alone an entire night. Before he left, he threw a handful of something that I couldn't see on the fire and the smell grew stronger, though the color and intensity of the flames never changed.

When he was out of the hut, I saw that he had a burlap sack over his right shoulder and a butcher's blade in his left hand.

'Cash or a long walk,' he said and pointed to the muddy road we came in on.

I pulled ten hundred-dollar bills from my pocket and gave them to him. He licked his thumb, counted the bills, and pushed them into his pocket.

'Mhh hm,' he said while looking over my face, and then he said, looking through me, 'better deal. Now, as far as I see it, you paid to, how you said, tell da story of a snake hunta in da bayou. An' in orda ta tell da story of a snake hunta in da bayou, you gotta watch a snake hunta in da bayou. Now, dat don't mean talkin' to him, an' it don't mean interruptin' him neitha. From dis point on, if I's deem you need ta know abou' dis o' dat—if I's deem you ta move here o' dare, I's tell ya plain an' simple. Are we clear?'

Obviously, this wasn't what I thought I was paying for, nor had I made any terms at the outset, either, before I got in his vehicle in town or before I gave him the money, but most people I had worked with were always eager to speak about their trade, profession, ceremonies, rituals—whatever. Otha was not, nor did he wish to speak about anything unless it was on his terms, and he made this more than abundantly clear with both his words and his actions. The whole time he had been speaking, I had been watching his grip on the blade in his left hand. The hand looked almost completely at ease by the way he carried it, except his knuckles were ghost white, which meant he had been holding it with an extreme tension despite any other indications. Of course, as the night went on, I found out that that's just the way he held a blade—it didn't matter if he was speaking, walking, sitting staring at the sky or swamp—but at the time I thought it was a threat.

Naturally, I was upset. This man had charged me quite a bit of money to refuse to do or say anything and, on top of that, he was threatening me, but what could I say? Could I say, 'Hey, that's not fair, I can't work a piece out under these conditions'? No. Of course not. So I nodded and we walked into the shallow marshes behind his cabin.

And we walked and we walked and we walked deeper and deeper into the swamp. After a time, I began to feel confused. I knew that it must have been getting later in the day, as we must have been walking for the better part of several hours, but the half-light of the canopy's shade never seemed to change. That, coupled with the feeling that the temperature was only getting hotter, and not by a degree or two, but by ten or fifteen, seemed altogether unreal to me. The Amazon was never like that; neither was Indochina or the Indian subcontinent.

Still, we pressed on. I assumed he was trying to wear me out, but I no longer cared. I guess, in a way, if that was his goal, he succeeded. I neither cared nor wondered about where we were going or if we were going anywhere or if we would ever get there. I was just along for the journey.

There's a strange rhythm to the swamp, a warm time that wraps you around itself again and again. It's kind of like a thickness that's felt as a state of being rather than a tangible width that can be measured by a ruler or gripped by a hand, and this swamp was no different. The same feeling crept into every thought, met you around every corner. I give my indifference to any danger I might have been facing at that point to the swamp's singular feeling. This man could have done me harm, and I could have felt afraid, rather than angry, when I saw his grip on the knife or after we had been walking for a while, but I didn't feel afraid, and as time went on, I only became less concerned about the circumstances of our journey and more interested in the man before me. I felt like I didn't understand him at all, but, more than that, I couldn't begin to imagine anyone who could.

His gait in the swamp was certain and steady, yet he seemed to float through the muck and mud. In shallow water, his footsteps made no perceptible ripple, and his silence was absolute. That is, he made no noise brushing against a tree, fern, or patch of bush. His silence carried a weight in its midst.

Then, before us, without my noticing, was a small wooden boat tethered to a stump. I would almost call it a canoe, but I guess its dimensions made it more of a boat—maybe eight foot by four foot, five foot? Long enough for a man and a half to lie from stern to bow and wide enough to sit two thin men side by side on either of the two six-inch-thick seating slats.

'Here,' Otha said and pointed to the back of the boat.

I got in without reply and he pushed the boat out a few feet and climbed onto the other seat.

We were face to face for the first time in what I thought must have been over two hours, and I saw a look of complete absorption on his face. Every tension line, every hair on his head, was poised on what looked like the balance point between anticipation and apprehension. I was transfixed by the power of his expression, so much so that I spoke my next thought aloud without realizing I had done so until I overheard myself.

'How long was that walk really...' I said.

'Thirty, forty-five minutes,' Otha said without shifting his attention from the swamp.

'That can't be,' I said, now conscious of what I was saying.

I waited a moment for him to respond again, but he just kept staring out onto the swamp. After a while, he slowly lifted the two oars from the bottom of the boat, placed them in their oar locks, and started to row into the murky water.

I remained quiet as the fatigue from the walk continued to build. When I first sat down, I was happy to be off my feet, which I thought was odd, as I was used to walking all day across the savannahs of Angola or the tundra of Greenland and not feeling very tired at all. But as I sat there, I just became more and more tired. Otha must have guessed, because he kicked me a canteen from under his seat. I took a few sips and placed it back on the floor of the boat.

Then I started making mental notes of what I wanted to talk about for the piece I'd write. So far, nothing much had really happened. The color bits about the setting, the temperature, the atmosphere were easy. I'd written about swamps a couple times before, and, like I said, they're all pretty much the same. As for Otha, I still wasn't sure what I'd say, and, the more I tried to think about it, the less I had, or rather, the less I could focus on.

In the years that have passed, when I've thought about it, I've wondered if there wasn't some organic compound that acted as a hallucinogen in the area that made me lose track of time, feel exhausted, and lack the ability to focus—it makes sense, but I've talked with several horticulturalists about the area, and to their knowledge there wasn't anything that could have caused that, unless there was something in the water he gave me, but I had already started to feel strange well before that. Anyway, as you can see, I've turned this over in my mind quite a bit and I always end up running the same way—in circles. So, for lack of a better way to describe the feeling, it was like oxygen deprivation in the death zone—roughly over 26,000 feet. You run into that kind of problem on Everest, K2… Shishapangma… Anyway, you feel like you're in complete control of your mind and body, but you know you're not thinking as clearly as you want—you're missing things that seem obvious but somehow escape you. And your body seems like it's moving somewhat out of sync with how you think it should be working. Similarly, I also couldn't think as clearly as I'd have liked to in that swamp, and my body wasn't responding with as much strength as I felt it should. At the time, I didn't think about it because I couldn't, but in retrospect I often wonder how, at practically sea level, something like that could happen. I don't know. I still don't know, but something like that was what was happening, so I decided to switch to my hand-held tape recorder, since I didn't think I'd remember all of what was happening.[2]

I pulled it out, waved it to Otha to see if he'd have a problem, and he didn't respond for a moment, and then he nodded, so I took it as a sign that he was agreeing to an interview, pushed record, and placed it on the floor of the boat. I had enough

---

2 Here, concurrently with the narrator speaking for 36 seconds, I hear the sound of footsteps coming down a hallway and walking toward the microphone. They seem to be four to six sets of heavy shoes, probably boots, covered with mud, cement, or some other gristly, viscous substance, as the sounds are not crisp, but spongy.

batteries and enough tapes for 80 hours of recordings. Since I knew I wouldn't be gone more than a day, I was over-prepared, but you can get hung out to dry in situations like that—dead batteries, faulty tapes—so it's important to be careful.

And now, I just have to laugh, because at this point, I was ready for an in-depth interview, and yet, I couldn't think of a single question to ask. I wanted to find out as much as I could about this man who lived alone in the swamp, hunting snakes, but I couldn't. I wanted to write about the struggles of his life, like all the adventuresome struggles in all the lives I had written about before, but I couldn't think beyond that desire. It was like a hand was pushing on a box that was my conscious mind and all of the thoughts within it—and not a single thought could escape.

So, instead of having the interview that I wanted, I just sat there and stared at his hands. Those leathery palms that looked like pieces of manila paper that had been crumpled and uncrumpled a thousand times—a hundred thousand, a million times or more. All the while he just sat there, rowing to the left of this tree or the right of that shoal without ever looking behind him, steering the hunt certainly with those steady, ancient hands.

And then he stopped.

The boat slowed as he slipped each oar through the oar locks and placed each oar back in the boat and then returned the blade to his left hand with the same easy tension I had noticed at the beginning of the day, except this time he closed his eyes.

'It's gon' be a long night,' he said and then became very still.

I noticed that the twilight of the canopy still hadn't started to fade, but almost became more… vibrant. I knew that sunset was around 9 p.m. where we were, but I felt certain again that, somehow, many more hours should have elapsed than must actually have passed.

Now, there in the boat on that Louisiana swamp with the old snake hunter, I began to experience everything in my surroundings becoming more vivid. The grays were grayer and the greens greener and every sound became distinct. I could hear this bush rattle or that splash of the water or that animal sound I couldn't identify.

In retrospect, I do think this may have been drug induced, as enough time since the point at which I sipped his canteen had passed that I could have been starting to hallucinate. It was reminiscent of a certain type of trip I've had with shamans in Thailand. Specifically, when I was on assignment with Bianca doing a piece on the effects of the ritualistic ceremonies of indigenous peoples on real mental health outcomes. That is, if there was any correlate between these practices and real psychological healing. You know, in the same way that religious counseling, prayer, and meditation can produce a measurable therapeutic effect—increased relaxation measured by, like, decreased heart rate, decreased activity in the brain's stress centers and so on. The way we were going about this was by following a group of 25 or so people and several researchers from the ceremonies performed by a shaman to a laboratory and back again several times over the course of a few weeks. It was a great idea, except a few of the shamans said we wouldn't be allowed in to see them perform any of the rites and rituals unless we first agreed to undergo the procedure ourselves. This was no problem for either of us, so we went on our own after we had flown into Kamphaeng Phet in order to be ready to start observing and taking notes the following day. The rickshaw ride to the shaman's house was bumpy and fast, and we were both very jet-lagged, but we managed to put on smiles for the healer. When we walked into the gray cinder block home, we were actually greeted by a group of men—about ten, the entirety of the healers that would be working with the test group over the next few weeks. They said that they were very excited to see us, and then they told us to sit. We sat down, and then they told us to stand up. This happened three times, and then they spoke to themselves in a heavily accented dialect that neither of us could understand. Finally, we were told that they could, in fact, work with us, but that we'd have to head out into the jungle right away. So, we followed them into that hot, green mess for several hours—all while Bianca and I watched the sweat stains build across their canvas polo shirts, jean shorts, and khakis. When we arrived at where we were going, the group just stopped and then we stood quietly for several minutes. Th—

[…radio silence, dead audio for two minutes and 53 seconds, then the hum of low frequency feedback for another 16 seconds…]

By that time, my experience was that I was walking up a winding, completely white staircase. My steps were steady and after I rounded each step, another appeared. This continued for some time before I noticed there was also a sound associated with the vision—it was the voice of what I took to be a female flight attendant over an intercom system. She kept saying, 'You're almost there. You're already there. You're almost there. You're already there.' I have no idea how long this continued, but then I found myself in the sky, an endless, infinite sky of clear pale blue in every direction. Above, below, in front of me, to either side and to the left and right of me—and, I was falling. Well, sort of. I could also have been moving up or forward or backward or to either side—any direction really, because, although I knew that I was moving, I had no idea in what direction. I was almost frightened, but there was nothing to fear—no ground, no objects, no anything, just an infinite pale blue sky of pure impossibility. Self-luminous, I remember the only thought I had was, 'Where is the sun?' And then, 'The sun is the sky.' I have no explanation or idea what that was, and then I was on a beach, watching seagulls beneath several clouds. I remember sitting up to watch one of them dive at the ocean, and then I was in a bed in the cement building where we had met all the shamans. To my left was Bianca smiling at me. She said, 'Did you find what

you were looking for?' I asked her what it was that I was looking for. She said, 'I really don't know.' I then told her all about
what I had seen and asked her what she had experienced. She
said she'd had a long conversation with her mother, who had
passed away many years before, about happiness, comfort, and
the importance of gardening. At the end of it, the thing that
was most clear in my mind was that intensification of sensory
feeling—the aware, vivid aspect of the visions, like the ones that
I might have been having in the swamp, except the ones I had in
Thailand had progressed into full-on hallucinations. This thing
happening in the swamp plateaued pre-visuals, with everything
very vivid, but concrete. If I were to guess, though—and I try
not to guess about these events—I think it was just the intensification of that feeling of not being able to think that had started
a bit before, in the swamp. Less thought led to a more primal
understanding of my surroundings.

Then I felt the fear. It wasn't about anything except for the
situation itself. When the world becomes too vivid, and you
try to think as hard as you can and no thoughts come while
you're completely conscious, your external surroundings start
to dominate your internal world, and internalizing that swamp
was—look at me—every time I talk about this my hands begin
to shake.

The rustle of the water to my left climbed into my sense of
balance and made everything unstable. The heat surrounding
every surface, every pore replaced my ability to feel the limits
and dimensions of my body, making me believe I was both
larger than I have ever been and suspended over the water and
smaller than I can remember having been as a child. And the
sensation of some movement in the tress over here or the marsh
ahead erased my emotions as I recognized them and filled me
with a sharper sense of something I can only call my failure
to recognize my experience as a defined being—a failure to

understand how I can exist at all and to feel the impact of that paradox in its entirety.

I felt such unrelenting fear in these experiences that I was certain I was going to give myself a heart attack.

The world was climbing inside me and it was desperately intent on taking away from me whatever part of myself I held from it. It was... ... ... it was... ... ... it was nothing I can give a name. And this went on for hours until, after being there for a thoughtless infinity, I started to forget about what my life had been before that experience. I started to become the cracking of the branches above me and the stench of the bog in my lungs.

Then *FWHAP!*

I saw before me in perfect detail Otha open his eyes, raise the blade, and bring it down against the side of the boat in one instantaneous motion. Then he pulled the largest reptile I have ever seen, fist over fist, into the bottom of that boat. It was thirty or so feet long with red and yellow stripes the length of its body. I watched him do this in complete silence and then he paused, holding the stump of the snake's body where the head had been over the edge of the boat. In my memory, the sound of the blade's crashing against the metal hull of the boat was still ringing at a faint echo as the blood poured over Otha's knuckles and his face contorted into a perfect fixation. Then I heard him speak:

'Dey come fo' da blood,' he said as it trailed over the side of the boat and fell into the obsidian water. 'Dey all come fo' da blood.'

And after that, he was silent again. He held the body for a moment longer, let it fall back into the boat, and resumed his vigil, blade in hand and eyes closed.

Five minutes could have gone by or five hours. In the total darkness of that night and my complete inability to gauge time, eons could have passed or instants.

I heard the water move from time to time, but almost nothing else, and anything else I did hear, I can't remember, except for Otha's speech. At some point, I just heard him speaking:

'You's a silly breed, boy. A silly, silly breed. I remembah as a child, a young thing seein' a man come 'round for my uncle and some of my uncle's friends akskin' to see deys music, akskin to tape deys words. And deys all said, yessir, you can have my words, but dey won't be da words you hear today. What you hear today stays with dis country, stays with dis land. Da rest is just a ghost in a dat dare tin can radio a yours. And da white man said, 'I undastand.' And he and his friends took deys recordings an' moved on. You bein' here reminds me a deese things. You here searchin' reminds me a dat way. Dat kind of man who wants to see the soul of another man's world without buyin' da hardships dat come wit dat kind of understandin'. You can't learn how to sweat da whip blows witout slavin' ova da cotton. And you can't pick da cotton witout standin' in da field every long day. And you can't undastand what happens in dis type a world witout livin' dis type a way. You undastand me, boy? You gonna undastand.'

Then he made a noise like a hyena, something like a laugh I've never heard another man make and then I felt no fear, no confusion... but something like peace. Quiet and dark and almost... almost womb-like.

I could have fallen asleep, but from time to time I heard the blade against the side of the boat and the gong-like echo that followed each blow.

The next thing I remember, I woke up with Otha pulling the boat back up onto the edge of the marsh we had pushed off from the day before, except there weren't any snakes in the bottom of the boat, not even the one I had seen him kill.

'Where are the snakes?' I asked.

'What snakes?' he said.

'The ones you killed last night.'

Then he laughed a throaty, tobacco-scarred laugh that turned into a cough, and as he coughed, he looked very frail.

'Boy, I ain't catch no snakes. Las' night you fell asleep deader dan a rotted log while I check traps in da dark. If we's catch a snake, I don't knows about it,' he said and laughed again.

I remember thinking how fragile he looked in the morning light, then I remember thinking about how I could think again, and about how plain the light of the swamp was. It wasn't the full sunshine of an open field under a cloudless sky, but I could see everything in complete detail.

'How far are we from your cabin?' I asked.

Otha looked at me with complete confusion and pointed right in front of him.

Standing not ten feet to my left was a large cabin with bright green metal siding.

'When did I fall asleep?' I asked, staring at the cabin and then back at the boat and then back at the cabin again.

'Soon's yous got in da boat,' he said.

I burst into tears right in front of him and he ushered me into his home. The house had a 1950s décor and no fireplace. The A/C was turned way up. He explained it wasn't working properly, and that's why the place was so cold.

He fed me pie for breakfast, which was delicious, and then we got in the truck for him to drive me back to the diner. On the way, I checked the tape recorder, hoping to find the sound of the blade, hoping to find anything, but it just sounded like degraded tape. What I heard could have been a malfunctioning recording or it could have just been a defective tape.

I remember as I got out of the car at the diner, he said, 'Dare ain't always an easy explanation of a life.'

Not often is there a day that goes by where I don't find myself trying to explain that life.

[...radio silence, dead audio for one minute and 18 seconds, then soft scratching, probably a magnet near an amplifier creating a minimal Barkhausen noise...]

[Male, Age: 74–83, English Accent. Designation: "Englishman"]
[Englishman]: Height: 6'1". Weight: 175 lbs. Eye color: hazel. Myopia: None.

[Female, Tri-Accent]: Metric.

[Englishman]: Height: 1.85 meters. Weight: 79.4 kg.

[End Of Tape I]

779J.2314.PPJR
[Tape II]

Date recorded: Approx. 1998
Pure CrO2 coating
AC bias 88.1-99.2 kHz
mostly minimal hysteresis

[American]: It was my experience with Otha that led me to expand my circle of interest with respect to the type of story I pursued. I enjoyed adventure and I enjoyed journalism, in as much as I got to learn about others—their lifestyles, their habits, their interests, concerns, rituals—but Otha... changed my definition of *other*. *Other*, after that, meant anyone slightly further afield of whatever I thought *other* meant—that is, anyone who was truly beyond explanation.

I couldn't go after stories in the same way that I had before for the first few months after Otha, or rather, I couldn't go after the same stories with as much excitement as I had before. After the swamp, I couldn't get to sleep at night without thinking about that place, about what had or hadn't happened, about any of it.

Of course, after a while, after I had visited Everest's Base Camp once more and kayaked down an uninhabited stretch of the Amazon and investigated purported sightings of the extinct Tasmanian tiger, I returned to the swamp.

I went back to the diner. I followed the same roads. Except this time, I came to dead ends, access trails, and ditches where there had been paved roads, gravel drives, and county junctions that I had traveled with Otha.

I tried to find him again, but I couldn't even locate a single 'Dale' listed in the entire Louisiana Department of Wildlife, Fisheries, and Parks directory, and no one at the VFW had ever heard of anyone named Big Tilly. I even asked Julien about his notes to double check if I had missed anything, but he said that there had been a small storage fire and most of his old records, along with the ones concerning Otha, had been destroyed.

I was out of luck. I had no sources that could back my story up, no one to follow up with, and no leads. All I had were the memories, the scenes I played over and over again in my head at night. And then, eventually, I went back to sleeping without thinking about it. I decided that I had made the whole thing up, or that I must have fallen asleep, or that I must have thought Otha's house was in a different place than it was. However I justified it, I wrote it off and went back to work.

Of course, I always listened for offbeat material in my journalist friends' stories, but nothing ever grabbed my interest. In general, nothing about the experience stayed with me, except my interest in slightly stranger stories. I was the guy that would go spend six weeks in silence in the company of Carthusian monks to write about their absolutely quiet lives. Lives they lived behind thick abbey walls and vows of silence. Or the guy that would spend a week alone in a supposedly haunted Irish castle. Or the guy that would opt for taking a vision quest in New Guinea. Before, it had been more about the people in a different way. Now, it was more about their experience, and not just their experience from the outside, but their experience from the inside. I tried as best as I could to write about what I had lived, rather than what I saw was being lived. And it's a fussy distinction, maybe a useless one, but it was slightly different from the way I had approached my job before.

And then, I was at a market in Turkmenistan, meeting up with Julien. It was outside of Ashgabat and there were dozens of vendors. There were rugs—so many rugs—of all shapes and sizes in rich, dark colors, laid over sofas and chairs and tents. And between these almost endless displays of dyed and colored wool lay empty square lots of rusted car parts, herbal tea merchants, grocers, livestock, and kebabs of yogurt and meat. It was a bright, hot day and there were droves of people out.

We met for coffee at a makeshift café that had refrigerator boxes draped in bright linens for tables and wood crates spray painted black for seating. He was on his way to visit the Darvaza gas crater, also known as the 'Door to the Abyss,' and I had just finished spending a month traveling with a nomadic herding community, learning about their millennia-old ritualistic style of horsemanship for a breeding magazine. This kind of curiosity assignment was less and less Julien's thing. He was focusing more on human-interest pieces, but he knew I had been growing a reputation for the exact type of story he was getting out of. The type of story he had tipped me off about with the swamp. And while I listened to him fret about his assignment, he offhandedly mentioned something that caught my attention.

He said, 'It's like chasing the City of Dreams—the reader always expects more intrigue than is actually there.'

I asked him what he meant.

'It's a mirage,' he said. 'The burning pit in the middle of nowhere that's been burning for over twenty years is just that— a burning pit fueled by natural gas deposits, confirmed by a new series of geological surveys that state the fossil-fuel-rich soil will continue to burn for many more decades into the future—not that it is, or is anything remotely close to being, in fact, the Gates of Hell.'

'No,' I said, 'what do you mean by chasing the City of Dreams?'

'C'mon, you've been doing this type of thing now longer than I have. This is *exactly* up your alley. You really haven't heard of this?' he said, expecting me to laugh, but instead I just stared at him, waiting for him to go on.

'The City of Dreams,' he said, 'is an old myth in journalism. You really haven't heard of this?' he asked, emphasizing the *you* with a capital *Y* in his voice.

Whatever he was talking about, for whatever reason, struck me in a very odd way. My interest was inherent, instinctive, like a dog with a bone that keeps gnawing and gnawing until the bone is nothing but splinters in its mouth. At the time, I racked my brain for anything I could remember having read in newspapers or books or magazines—or overheard in passing conversations—and there was nothing, absolutely nothing. My memory was empty, blank.

'No,' I said, 'I really haven't—now tell me more.'

'The City of Dreams,' he said, 'is a myth in journalism that connects loose statements about dreams in relationship to a place from various historical sources. Dr. Livingstone's journal contains a passage about a "Plateau of Dreams" in relationship to cannibals he heard about in the mountains of Burundi. Napoleon's field notes mention a "Caravan of Dreams" in the heavy rain outside of Genappe before the battle of Waterloo. Cortés is fabled to have told a story to the King of Spain about a merchant in Tlaxcala who had been to the "Festival of Dreams." The list goes on. Even the Egyptians have hieroglyphs that can be translated as the "City of Sleeping Worlds." The point is, it's a myth—a mirage in the margins of conjecture and hearsay. People want it to be real, want it to be true, so they imagine they hear things about it or connect events or source materials to one another in selective or specific ways. Dr. Livingstone was in a malaria fever for most of his time in Africa. Napoleon could have been writing about his dreams the night before Waterloo. Cortés could have been embellishing a bedtime story for the Emperor of the New World—the hieroglyphs could just as easily be interpreted as talking about death, as the Egyptians were most of the time anyway. You get the point—it's not real, it's a dream.'

'Of course,' I said, finished my coffee, and paid for the both of us while I told him I had found it an interesting story. Then, before I left, I thought to ask him if he'd spoken to Bianca. He said that he had, and I asked how she was doing. He seemed nervous and said she was doing well. I understood, or thought I did, and said that if I should come up, to let her know that I said hello. He knew how hard the break-up was on both of us, and I assumed he didn't want to bring up any painful memories with her. I would have asked him to relay more—there was so much I wanted to tell Bianca, that I missed her warm, soft smell in the bed beside me, her turquoise and ruby jewelry on the windowsill, or the way she'd run two fingers down the side of my neck every time we'd meet—but that's not the type of message you send through a mutual friend. It's not fair, not to anyone, to be in that position. So, I told him it was good to see him and left the café.

The rest of the day before my flight, I thought about the swamp again. And, again, I forgot about it, the City of Dreams and everything that wasn't my current assignment, until I was called to the Walled City of Kowloon before its destruction in '93.

You've probably heard of it. I would be surprised if you haven't.

Kowloon was a hive of a city just outside of Hong Kong. It was a military fort until the late 1800s, when it became a refugee camp for displaced Chinese during the British occupation of Hong Kong—and then even more displaced Chinese during the Japanese occupation of WWII. As it was only ever meant as a temporary way station, its boundaries were small, and because of China's hundred-year contract with the British for the surrounding provinces, Kowloon never expanded. That, mixed with the fact that the refugees didn't want to leave in any of that turmoil, not to mention the Cultural Revolution, meant that more and more people sprawled over one another like ants—building their houses and walkways and shops on top of, through, beside, betwixt, and between one another until it became like a child's idea of how a city could be—without thought, without any impossibility. This structure attached here, this sewer trenched there, this alleyway going backward and forward and sideways and up and down until it had become and been and then become again a ladder, a tunnel, a street, a staircase, and a bridge. Dreamlike—it was truly dreamlike, but of course they were not all good dreams.

Naturally, because of its almost hyper-density, it became a breeding ground for prostitution, gambling, drugs—you name it, and eventually you could find it in the Walled City. Mostly lawless, it ended up being run by Triads, the ruthless, cult-like Chinese gangs that swore oaths of allegiance under blood sacrifices and were avoided by all those who could do so.

You see, I had been to the Walled City several times since the '70s and I wasn't afraid of it. Because of that, and maybe because I seemed like someone who could get by there for more than a few hours, I was sent to report on its final days.

I got there in June of '92 and its demolition started in March of '93. There was no relocation program—or almost none, anyway. Everyone's home, business, or place of leisure was worthless with a soon-to-pass expiration date, and I wondered if that's what it was like when Pompeii saw Vesuvius beginning to erupt. To say that it was a panic would be a disservice to how bizarre that panic was—orgies in the street, overdoses on rooftops, and everything in-between. I heard gunshots and laughter almost constantly that trip, and yet, I didn't really ever feel like I was in any real danger. In a way it was like the whole environment was a drug, no one was in control, no one was pulling the strings. Everyone was just another passenger making the best of a runaway train headed for the edge of an abyss. When all bets are off, it does strange things to the mind.

I interviewed retired couples who refused to move and were committed to going down with their homes, and businessmen from Hong Kong looking for their last thrills in the complex they knew as the City of Darkness.

It was there, in that chaos, that I encountered the graffiti. Four characters that plainly translated as, 'The City of Dreams,' and, beside them, an arrow, and then another and then another and then another. I followed arrows for two days into chasms and crevices and lofts and lean-tos, asking everyone I saw, 'Do you know who drew this? Do you know about the City of Dreams?' Of course, no one knew anything, but the arrows did stop. Actually, there were three separate sets of arrows—that I discovered—sprawling over and through the basements, the ground level, and the skywalks respectively—all terminating inside an abandoned textile factory. I say 'that I discovered,' because several other colors of arrows, in different, disconnected places, all seemed to point to the same space as well, but graffiti changed so quickly in the Walled City that large stretches of their trails had already been covered over. In all actuality, in order to find three complete trails there must have been dozens, maybe hundreds.

After discovering where they led, I tracked down the owner, or holding entity, rather, a Buddhist temple sandwiched between a dentist's office and a tattoo parlor.

I remember it was just an empty storefront, completely dark, with the characters *Buddha's Drawing Room* written above the place where there would have been a door. Within, I could only see the outlines of people receding into the shadows. They were sitting in cross-legged positions without moving or talking, presumably meditating.

I stood in front of the space in confusion for several moments before an old, thin man came into the alleyway, holding a string of beads. His shoulders were arched forward, and he held the beads lightly in his hands. He rubbed them in a way where he'd roll two forward then three back, then three forward and two back—over and over—all with his hands, never once watching them with his eyes. They moved… his hands moved like water over rocks or the wind through leaves, unthinkingly, unendingly.

He explained that this place was a kind of monastic retreat, that if I was interested in worship there were several other temples in the neighborhood in which I could pray, both ahead of me, behind me, above me, and below.

I told him I was looking for 'The City of Dreams.'

He mumbled something to himself in song almost before I had finished asking my question... two bars, I didn't really think about it, but it was... it was, 'are you the dreamer or are you the dream?'

'I'm sorry, I can't help you,' he said almost abruptly, yet still somehow calm, after he had finished rhyming to himself.

I told him that I had traced several trails through the city to a building that he or his collective owned.

'The Third Location,' he said and nodded to himself.

'I'm sorry?' I asked and he went on.

He said that it was the third location in sixty years that the Triads had asked him to prepare. He said that usually the Triads were ruthless, independent organizations, but that once, every twenty years, they came together under a single common cause—the City of Dreams.

I asked if he knew what the City of Dreams was.

He smiled and said that everyone knew what the City of Dreams was, but that no person could explain what it was to any other. He also said that it was gone, and that's why he couldn't help me.

'Does it have something to do with drugs, prostitution, high-stakes gambling?' I asked.

'For some,' he said and nodded, 'but not in the way that you mean.'

I asked if he could clarify.

'The City of Dreams,' he started, 'is different for everyone. And for everyone, it is also the same.'

'Does it have to do with dreams—with actual dreaming?' I asked.

'Oh, yes,' he said.

'So sleep is involved?' I asked.

'In a way,' he said.

Now, it's not hard to understand that, at this point, I was

more or less confused. Was this City of Dreams 'The' City of Dreams, the fabled City of Dreams, or—as I stood and thought about it—just a way for the Triads to experiment with how much money they could make by cooperating and then splitting the profits equally?

As I was going about it in the way that I was, I had no way of knowing, but I knew *exactly* why I was talking to the person I was talking to.

Religion is a powerful tool. Mao knew it, and the Triads, obviously, knew it as well. It works as an opiate, yes, but it also works as an incredibly sophisticated language. The reason I wasn't frustrated with any of this man's answers was because I knew he was telling me—with *extreme* precision—everything I wanted to know. I knew that because I had seen this hundreds of times before with dozens of different religions.

I've found that sometimes, particularly among religious people, beliefs can function as a sort of conversational shorthand. For example—a very basic example—in the West, the average man who wears the yarmulke knows more about the average man he meets on the street who does or doesn't, and vice versa. They know that the man with the yarmulke is Jewish, that he doesn't eat pork, that he observes a custom by wearing this garment—et cetera, et cetera, so on and so forth—a certain number of things can be known about him. This number, within the right setting, becomes even greater. Let's say that the same Jewish man were to meet another Jewish man in a synagogue—now each person knows even more about one another. They each know that they are observant of their faith, that they have invested in its tenents to some greater degree in meeting at the same time and place to celebrate its customs. Because of this, each person is better able to understand the other. In celebrating those same tenants, they can feel comfortable speaking... more deeply with one another in this other language—this language of beliefs and customs. Incidentally, in Judaism, this language is Hebrew. However, the language, itself, is meaningless compared to what is understood in the context of its use. When two people use it in the right setting, they are really talking about how they believe the same things, know those same things, let those same things seep into and out of their everyday lives, into and out of their experiences as a living being, into and out of their contexts for being alive. When those people talk, they are talking within the context of believing in a certain set of ideas about life, death—the nature of reality itself. The nature of that dialogue is reflected in more and more of their behavior at deeper and more committed levels, as that dialogue corresponds to how they interact, at the most basic levels of understanding and belief, with their world.

Do you see where I'm going?

So, when people of an even greater shared context get together, their language reflects those subtler nuances to a greater degree. When two rabbis meet or two Jesuit Priests or two Hindu yogis—they each are better able to translate the lived language of the other. Their conversation will be based on it—on these customs, beliefs, and contexts—to such a delicate and intricate degree that their exchange would be almost completely incomprehensible to anyone else. A casual observer would never be able to penetrate its complexity. In it, a nod could mean chastisement, censure, adoration, or devotion. A narrowing of the eyes could be ridicule, adulation, dismissal, or agreement. A modulation in tone, word choice, the pace of the conversation—everything in the context of those situations matters to the finest degree.

In this world, the world of an extremely refined shared context, understanding is a function of everything they were not only doing, but being. Their vocabulary is synonymous with their entire personality, which is synonymous with their understanding and beliefs.

This—this type of total language—was exactly what I felt like I was dealing with in the man from the shadowed abbey.

The two verses he had hummed to himself, the way he was half-answering my questions—his calm mannerisms in response to all of my inquiries—the reference to the third location; he was the member of an inner sanctum. In a very certain, very specific way, he was communicating with me.

The interesting thing is that I couldn't place his 'dialect'—the religion within which he was speaking. It wasn't as easy as saying, 'Hey, that's Buddhism. That sounds vaguely Buddhist.' As I said before, that's only the first level of the dialogue—like the man that wears the yarmulke. This was China, a land that had been influenced by Buddhism for over a thousand years. The entire culture was steeped, to some not small degree, in its customs. I knew there had to be more to what he was saying because he was giving me everything and nothing at the same time. The way he said what he said invited an answer in order to evade it. Of course, I went through the obvious sects: Mahāyāna, Gyeyul, Ritsu. Then, I went through some of the nuances I detected— Zen, of course, but also Vajrayana, Pudgalavada, Kagyu...

I'm no layman when it comes to most religions—learning customs is a large part of my job—but I also don't typically have to put together an entire belief structure from a short conversation. The best I could make of it, the way he talked about 'the dream'—the Buddhist belief that this world is just an illusion compared to Nirvana, Buddhist Heaven—wasn't in a strictly traditional sense, at least, not in any traditional sense that I had observed or seen. He was referencing something that was a dream, that was about dreaming, that had to do with real sleep, a real place and event that also could be seen as unreal. Basically, I needed to unpack what he was saying, and the most I could glean from it at the time was to infer that the thing, place, state we were talking about was something that was both the thing we were talking about and a metaphor for it or some unknown mixture or something like that... Something dense— really, really dense.

It was an inner sanctum I had not encountered. While I knew that Zen was a close cousin, I also realized that I could never intuit, let alone understand, everything I was being told. They were riddles. The man I was talking to was talking in riddles. In order to approach the riddles in a way that I might derive something of their meaning, I needed him to provide me with some purchase on the material, a grip I could cling to in order to begin to get a better feel for it.

That is why the Triads had employed this man. He was the perfect gatekeeper of the secret he was protecting in plain sight. A devotee of this completely esoteric religion, he was someone for whom the thing was so abstract and important that the Triads could be safe in knowing that it was completely hidden from anyone who wasn't initiated into its teachings.

So, I stood there and I thought—I thought about him, about Kowloon, about the textile factory, about dreams—about religions and contexts and everything I could put together about this thing.

Yes, I knew it was something to do with dreaming, but what? What did what I need have to do with the 'dream' or 'dreams' or 'dreaming'?

Yes, he was giving me riddles, but as I thought about it he, himself, became—more and more—the real riddle, the real thing.

I didn't really need him to give me any information about the City of Dreams, verbally, per se, but I did need him to give me a point of reference.

Knowing that anything that could draw the attention, literally, of the entire corrupt city of Kowloon to one place was going to have something to do with the Triads, I figured it would be too dangerous to try to break into the textile factory on my own, which is why I tracked down its owner.

I knew there was at least this connection to the Triads—to start from. The man in front of me had confirmed the unholy union between his religious organization and the group of vicious gangs that ran the city, a chilling and disturbing fact on its own. Though, I also knew they were using this man because of his simplicity, because of his blending into the mythology of the City of Dreams itself. That type of mythology takes faith, and faith, usually, at least in Buddhism, which I believed this faith was at least tangentially related to, was something that involved gentle, compassionate, and earnest beliefs. Had I asked for his prayer beads, his robes, or his life, I'm sure he would have given any or all of them in a heartbeat.

They were using a saint to guard a secret. It's hilarious. It's also genius. It is also easy to work with if you can understand how all of these things relate to one another.

I had to focus on yes or no questions and try something that could be suicide considering the Triads were secretive, entirely unforgiving, and completely involved in this thing.

I asked three questions.

'Does entering the city cost any money?'—'No.'

'Is money exchanged within the city?'—'No.'

'Can I see the factory?'—'Yes.'

You see, all three of these answers were problematic. The first two were perplexing—Triads are not public servants, nor are they superstitious. If money wasn't involved, what was? What were they getting out of it?

The third was a problem, because knowing the answer to the first two, I had to press on, and knowing the fever of bloodlust and insanity that had already taken the city in its final days, to press groups of mass murderers that held some secret between them almost holy seemed morbidly psychotic.

But, it was addictive, strangely addictive, to be in a position to find out even a little more about this city-riddle, maybe the same city-riddle that had haunted explorers for hundreds, if not hundreds of thousands of years.

So, I followed the man who followed the Religion of Dreams to that abandoned textile factory in that dying city.

And you know what? It wasn't even locked. The man opened the door with ease. Maybe it wasn't a secret. Maybe this whole thing was stranger than it seemed.

Whatever it was, I walked into the factory with a flashlight and scattered its light across the structure's frame—except there was no frame.

The space, cavernous and deep, was entirely empty. The whole thing, as far as the flashlight could shine—nothing.

It was disturbing to be in—to see a space so big and so black that it just swallowed the light in every direction, that it just took it like a vacuum in empty space. It was huge. I knew it was huge, but that darkness. It pressed against you, pushed at you. When I think of it, and I know it doesn't make any sense, I see an image… or I have this idea of an image—that of a shadow's shadow, the darkness cast by darkness. That's how black it was, how close it felt. And in that space, all noise was hushed. I couldn't hear any of the hum of the city. I could barely hear the sound of my own footsteps.

There was the dented and dinged sheet metal floor and that was it—that's all I saw, at least until I started to walk around, and then, after half a minute to either side, I could see the metal walls and steel beams. It took another minute and a half to reach the back, and then I started to walk the whole perimeter.[3]

For a long while, there was only the metal of the floors, the siding, and the beams, and then I noticed it, the faint and some-how luminous smell of saffron in the atmosphere. I say luminous because when I think about it, even now, I see it as a blue faded vapor in my mind. I can taste it, see it, feel its light—a warm, sweet, caring feeling.

---

3   Here, concurrently with the narrator speaking for ten seconds, I hear several doors open and close. Two of wood, three of metal.

It was so strange and so rich for such a faint smell that it produced a type of blending of my senses, a type of synesthesia.

Drugs—drugs were my first thought. It must have been some kind of opiate mist. The man who had brought me there must not have known about the money and how the Triads hid it, or he was in such deep denial that he had hidden it from himself. He seemed very much like a trusting man. It wasn't difficult to see how in either case he could have been deceived.

Then I kicked something soft. I pointed my flashlight to the ground, and there were dozens of piles of deep-ochre-colored powder about three inches tall and six inches wide.

Jackpot, I thought. It obviously looked like saffron, but it had to contain opiates. Either it was the opiate base itself for whatever I was smelling in the atmosphere or trace opiates from the atmosphere would have landed on the piles themselves, proving the whole thing was a drug operation.

At the time, it didn't strike me as strange that I had stumbled upon several hundred thousand dollars' worth of opiates cut with saffron and laid in piles on the floor of an abandoned textile factory in the lawless City of Kowloon, but it had been a strange few days. I scooped a bunch of the powder into my bag and left.

Curious to see what he'd say, on the way out, I asked the devotee of the Religion of Dreams one last question:

'Where did the city go and why did it leave?'

He smiled and said, 'All dreams must end and they return to the place of all dreaming.'

'Right,' I said, and left Kowloon.

On my way to the airport in Hong Kong, I left the powder with a friend at a British chemical lab and asked them to screen the results—a full write-up, everything they could tell me.

I left the city and slept like a baby on the plane after having stayed up for almost a week straight. For two months, I went back to work, satisfied that I had pursued what I could in

Kowloon, certain of the results I'd eventually receive from the lab screening of the powder.

After I got back from a trip to the Arctic, where I did a piece cataloging several of the failed expeditions approaching the ice cap from Greenland, I saw that I had gotten the results from Hong Kong.

I opened the box and took out the screening along with a small pouch of the powder.

Nothing in it—saffron, a little dirt, nothing else. There was nothing in the toxicology screen to suggest any form of opioid, let alone any other type of hallucinogen—natural or manmade.

They found so little, in fact, that they had placed a note at the bottom of the last sheet of results, asking if I knew where they could get a sample of it in the wild, as they hadn't yet come across that strain of saffron crocus and wanted to know if I had any particular attachment to the naming rights for the strain.

So, I did my bit for investigative journalism. I opened the bag, laid a thin line of ochre powder on the table in front of me, and rolled up a dollar bill.

I did that three times—nothing. I could vividly remember the way that I felt in that place. I could remember all the ways in which I could sense the blue nebula, but I couldn't have that same experience again. It wasn't there. This pile of powder in front of me was just saffron and dirt—a new strain of saffron, but just saffron and dirt.

Of course, I couldn't return to Kowloon. There was a moratorium on anyone entering or leaving. Those who fled had outstayed their legal welcome and were subject to prosecution, and those that entered were presumed to be looters of property of the state and were subject to prosecution just the same.

So, instead, I did some research and I bought some source materials, or copies of source materials, on people's descriptions of this place that did and didn't exist—this place that kept becoming bigger and bigger, stranger and stranger in my mind—the City of Dreams.

I entertained ideas of searching for it—out there—on my own. I had the skills and the ability to track and survive, but there was nowhere to search. There wasn't more than a name on the wind in a dozen locations spread throughout history.

I wondered what the religious man had meant when he said 'The Third Location.' Had that meant that the city had been there, in Kowloon, three times? Had it been near there three times? Had the man himself known of and organized three remote places that it had been held on the globe?

And then, I found myself thinking about the city itself more and more. Was it a type of caravan? Did it have buildings? Were there parks and gardens? I thought about it so much that I started to dream about it. For months, I dreamt of mastodons, King Arthur's court, Sun Tzu, the Spanish New World, the Arctic, Atlantis—all in the context of this place I had never been. I've never experienced or seen anything—not drugs, not women, not power—act on the mind the way the idea of that place did on my own. My imagination couldn't place this thing in a time or a place, so in each location it would be new and different and strange.

In prehistory, it was a city of yurts a mile wide and ten stories high. Mastodons rode into the city, hauling great totem pole statues made, in some way, from fog, ash, and sand. In Roman England, it was a stone building a hundred yards long by a hundred yards wide with a long, low thatched roof. King Arthur would send knights into the building in search of the Holy Grail many times, never to hear of their return. In mainland China, it was a moving battlefield that Sun Tzu assaulted a thousand times, never to conquer its cunning. In the New World, it was a forest city in the canopy along the Amazon. Happy children would carry messages into the city and return the next day as sober adults.

These dreams, they were all so vivid and all so strange that I could spend all day telling you the details of each and every one, but their important details were all the same—I could never see inside the city. I could only walk around outside it.

Of course, this was just my subconscious telling me how obsessed I had become, but again, with time, I started to forget the intrigue of just another bizarre, unexplained phenomenon and began rationalizing its novelty. After a while, I decided it was probably just an elaborate diversion set up by the Triads to misdirect attention away from some other illegal activity. There was no City of Dreams in Kowloon, just the remnants of some carnival or pseudo-religious festival that served to distract enough of the Walled City's people from their last minute revelries so that something big enough to warrant inter-Triad cooperation might take place, like a heavy weapons deal, a large shipment of human cargo, or a high-profile hit.

I continued to feel that way until I received a note in the mail from Julien. In it, he mentioned that Bianca was glad he and I had gotten a chance to talk, that she wanted to say hi and that she was happy for me in regards to the direction my career was taking. From that, I took that she still didn't want to talk, but I was glad, in a way, that she wanted to say hi. There was that and then a mention of my and Julien's meeting in Turkmenistan. He referenced our conversation about the city and included a clipping from a small newspaper in Pofadder—a remote village in South Africa—to reemphasize his point that, occasionally, there was some kind of allusion to such a place, but that it was always just a hoax.

The spelling in the article was atrocious, as was the obvious panhandling for 'tips' on the offer to provide maps to its 'exact' location from local street vendors—obviously the people who had taken the ad out—but it didn't matter. I was on a plane to Cape Town that afternoon.

On the flight, I planned the fastest route to the village and kept hoping the city, whatever it was, was still there. The paper's clipping didn't include a date, just the name of the city where maps were available. The postmark date for the letter itself was only a week old, so it seemed possible that I could make it there in time.

When I got off the plane I rented a truck right away, my excitement outweighing the tiredness I felt from not having slept on the flight. I filled it with three ten-gallon drums of extra fuel, some provisions, and a rifle. Then I drove and drove and drove. For the first bit, it was still light out, and the light along the water was comforting; then I turned inland, and that's when things became more, well, interesting.

A few hours north of Cape Town, I came along a stretch of empty two-lane highway hemmed in by low-hanging brabejum trees. They were round and green and lush in the light from my headlights, until I started to see hands extending beyond their branches. At first, I thought the trees had hands, and then I saw more and more of them—all small and held palm-up. As I slowed down, I saw they were the hands of children, dozens of children lining the side of the highway—all in a row to my right. When I looked to my left, there were no children, and when I looked back, the ones I had seen were gone. My eyes were heavy and felt like dry glue when I blinked, but I had no idea I was *that* tired. I was shaken, definitely, but I assumed I had been imagining things in that kind of aimless way. You know—like how if you look at clouds long enough, or the pattern of a quilt, or the wind in the trees, you start to see things? I just assumed it was something like that. I was tired, I had been staring at the highway for hours and, at that moment, I realized I was hungry. So, I pulled to the side of the highway and ate a type of barbecue I picked up from a street vendor outside of the gas station in the city. I remember it tasted really good, and then I remember the sound of elephants calling in the dark on the other side of the two-lane highway. They started wailing, louder and louder, until they suddenly stopped and I started to feel the ground shake. I knew enough to start the truck, floor it, and hope to God that I could outrun the stampede. As I pulled away—pedal to the metal—I saw a pack of lions cross the road behind me. When their heads turned in my direction, their eyes shone bright yellow in the glow of my taillights. They just stood there watching me as I shot into the distance. Whether they were chasing the elephants and the elephants had steered clear of the highway or I was hallucinating from some combination of stress, jet lag, and sleep deprivation, I don't know. I do know that their eyes were beautiful. They were sharp and curious and... I don't know. They were beautiful...

The rest of the night, almost nothing happened. It was just the mountains, the stars, and the arid planes. When dawn finally crept over the horizon on that last narrow dirt road, Pofadder came into view, and I was very, very tired.

When I pulled into the village, the sky was cloudy and it was windy. I asked several people if they could tell me who had taken out the ad. No one would talk to me. Everyone looked at me with suspicion and moved, more or less quickly, away. Eventually, after I asked several other street vendors, one of them pointed in the direction of a man.[4]

Barely on the edge of town—arguably, a little farther out than that—I found a sole newspaper stand that sold individual cigarettes, half-used pencils, old maps, and broken penknives. The only thing indicating that it was a newspaper stand at all were the walls. They were covered in *The Sowetan, Die Son, Ilanga Langesonto, The Johannesburg Times,* and a dozen others. It was a truly impressive collection for such a rural area, except that almost all of them were out of date. Some by a few weeks, others by months or years. One at the back seemed to be announc-

---

4   Here, concurrently with the narrator speaking for six seconds, I hear two or three flies buzzing around the microphone.

ing the end of the Vietnam War. And then there was the man who ran it. He was a young-ish looking African man with white hair. I say young-ish looking because as I approached he looked muscular and, although his face was downcast at the counter in front of him, it looked like it was smooth and without wrinkles.

When I asked if he was the man selling maps to the City of Dreams, he looked up from the counter.

His eyes—the *irises* of his eyes—were milk white. The man was blind.

Of course, this posed very problematic for a man who wanted to get accurate topographical information. I hesitated, but since he was the only person left to talk to, I asked the same question again. He said, '*Hakuna zaidi*,' which is Swahili for, 'no more.'

I asked if he had been to the city—*Hakuna zaidi*.

I asked if he had made the map—*Hakuna zaidi*.

I asked if he knew where it had gone—*Hakuna zaidi*.

I asked if I could buy a map—*Hakuna zaidi*.

I was going to ask if he could take me there, but before I could say anything else, he stood up and narrowed his eyes at me.

Now, it's extremely unnerving when a blind man narrows his eyes *at* you. If it had been in some other direction, if it had felt like he had been looking to the left or right of me—even by an inch—I would have felt something less than primal fear, but he just stood there with his empty gaze leveled at my eyes. He stared at me for maybe three or four seconds and then he walked out in front of his stand, bent down, and picked up a handful of dry earth. Then he stood up and stared right at me again and held out his other, empty, hand. I thought he was gesturing for me to give him my hand and I guessed correctly, because as I gave it to him, he held the earth over my palm and let it slip through his fingers. Before a single grain of sand touched my palm, it had scattered in the wind.

'*Hakuna zaidi*.'

It was a convincing gesture, because I knew I wouldn't find the City of Dreams there. I knew this man knew what he was talking about, and I knew that this was all the information I was ever going to get from him.

I refueled my truck and went home.

Months passed, and I occupied myself with work—going on expedition after expedition—reporting on attempts at unclimbed peaks in Patagonia, deep cave diving in Colombia—wreck exploration in the South China Sea.

Since I knew quite a bit about these things from having done them myself in my youth, and from all of the reporting I had done—from new ice climbing routes in the Yukon, extreme whitewater kayaking in South America, the latest BASE jumping spots in Scandinavia, to the latest and lowest deep-sea depths that oil welders were working at—I would often be offered extra pay as a consultant if I did some of the climbing, diving, charting—whatever. I *never* did this. It's stupid and reckless when a new climbing route or BASE jumping spot is being explored in any way, and I had, outside of calculated risks, stopped being as stupid and reckless as I had been when I was young, but those times—those offers I had been given after South Africa—I accepted them just to try to forget about the City of Dreams, just to sleep a little easier. To be too exhausted to think after days or nights spent burning adrenaline at both ends.

I did this for maybe six months before I heard, for the third and final time, about the elusive city.

The final time, Julien called me from Tsogttsetsii, a small town in Mongolia, and told me that he had recently heard about a 'Sleeping City.' He was on assignment doing a piece on some of the preservation efforts around the Khongoryn Els—the Singing Dunes—and he said that he had seen people, about 15 or 20 in total at different times over the past day, head by his camp on their way north. When he asked several of them where they were going, they said things like 'The Field of Sleep' and 'The Worlds of The Sleeping City.' Of course, it was just another anecdote to him, a joke, really, but knowing me and my pursuit of the truly unfamiliar, he called and told me about it anyway—in case I thought it might be worth pursuing.

Again, I was on a plane later that day.

Before I left, I asked him to chart a map where he had seen them last and to rent me camels and provisions to cart me there. He asked if I planned to go north into the desert after them. Without hesitation, I said yes.

The whole flight was torturous. Knowing that I had missed the city twice before, once within a matter of days, my stomach was in knots with anxiety, hope, and desire.

Again, when I got off the plane, I was exhausted, but my friend had come through, and I had everything I needed.

I reimbursed him for what he had paid for, got in the truck, and started looking over his map. North of the dunes is a wasteland—a massive wasteland the size of your palm on a map.

I wasn't looking forward to finding my way through high wind and high heat with no clear idea of where I was going, but I knew that I had to go.

Was it dangerous?—Yes.

Could I get lost?—Absolutely.

Was there a possibility I could die?—Almost certainly.

If my mother had begged me to go back and forget about it, would I have? No—not on your life, hers, or anyone else's.

I was going to get to that city or as close as I could, or I was going to go mad.

When the truck stopped, I quickly inspected the camels—good teeth, good feet, clean coats—and I headed north.

[Indeterminable Sex, Indeterminable Accent]: Did any of the camels have markings?

[American]: You mean like brands?

[Indeterminable Sex, Indeterminable Accent]: No, other features—specifically along the throat.

[…radio silence, dead audio of nine seconds followed by a shuffling of feet for nine seconds followed by the faint howling of dogs for nine seconds, and then a hushed whispering for nine seconds…]

[American]: As I think about it, no. No markings. One camel was heavier than the others. Another had a grayer sheen to its coat, but nothing like that.

[Indeterminable Sex, Indeterminable Accent]: Proceed.

[American]: So the heat died down quickly as twilight set in, and I wrapped a yak-skin coat over my shoulders. I watched the stars come out one by one on the purple, blue, and gold horizon as I climbed due north over the sands.

I remember it reminded me of the time Bianca and I were in the middle of the Pacific on the northernmost island of Tuvalu. We were doing a piece on the validity of certain folk tales, and the editor of the magazine wanted us to make sure we tested the most obscure hearsay. This took us to a small island nation where the editor had once heard natives describe drifting between islands with the tide. I didn't doubt that it was possible, but when we got there, we found out that the distance between the two islands we were to test was over thirty miles. We were also told that several people's great-grandfathers and great-grandmothers had completed the journey just on their backs—with nothing else. When I asked if anyone there had done it themselves, everyone said no, but that they were sure it could be done. Fortunately, when the editor had first heard this particular anecdote, she had understood the indigenous peoples to be referring to a voyage made by a small handmade craft. This wasn't especially encouraging either, but it was a hell of a lot more encouraging than floating on our backs in the dead of night over miles and miles on a superstition. Of course, we took a radio and some other equipment, but we weren't allowed to bring paddles or a motor. If we had, we could have been accused of just rowing or motoring the distance, and that wouldn't have proven anything. No, we were pretty much on our own when we left that beach with the evening tide. In principle, the theory was that if we left on full-moon low tide, it would pull us out far enough so that when we got caught up in the following morning's high tide, it would push us the rest of the way to the next island. That, and that the ocean currents between the two would keep us on a fairly steady course.

So, Bianca and I packed a day's worth of food and water just in case and pushed off the beach in a raft the locals made out of palm trees. As the stars rose over the horizon, I saw the same display as I did in that desert. They pulled themselves out of the darkening twilight and shone in simple brilliance over a monotonous expanse.

I remember both equally well, as they were the only things to look at until the moon rose over the ocean. Bianca and I watched most of it in silence. The dark waves lapped against the bright sky, and the bright sky reflected at angles on the white tips of the water. Neither of us ever got sea sick, so we just drifted between the two infinities, measuring the passing of time by the height of the moon. When we did speak, it was mostly about our speed or probable coordinates. You see, when we worked together, we often talked very little. It was our job to notice what was happening, to look at what was taking place, record it, and then attempt to write about it in an interesting way. We just happened to both work better in silence. Then, after a while, when the wind began to change, the conversation did as well. She said something in the way she always said things, things I only ever half-understood, but that I guessed at well enough most of the time.

'When the sea changes, do you?' I remember she said, almost too quietly for me to hear. In fact, I'm not sure she meant for me to hear the question at all. Sometimes she thought about things she didn't realize she was saying, only to be surprised when

I responded to them. Still, I wasn't sure if this was an instance like that or not, so I asked what she meant.

She said, 'Do you think of your life more like driftwood or more like an island?'

I thought about it for a long time, and then I said that, in a way, I thought of it as both, like an island of driftwood or a place that was sometimes an island, sometimes driftwood.

She smiled and ran two fingers along my neck and kissed me, then she went back into her own world. Whether she meant for me to hear that first question or not, I doubt I'll ever know. But from then on for several hours, she just stared at the horizon. And as that was her way, I didn't really think anything about it till the sky began to cloud over and the sea started to become more choppy. For a while, she stared at the uneven waves, then, as it began to rain, she started trying to figure out our exact position. I knew that the sun was almost on the horizon, but as the clouds were dark it looked almost as dim as the night had been. I also had a feeling that if it was going to happen, if we were going to make it, that in a few short moments, we'd see the island.

So I said, 'Let's ride it out.'

And she pointed out we could sink.

I said, 'We'll make it. This time we'll make it.'

'What if we drift?' she asked.

And I just smiled and pointed at the horizon through the gray, misty light. 'We all die someday. We don't all get such a sight.'

She laughed in a wild way. 'Look at you,' she said, pointing at my posture—at my blind confidence on a small raft *in the middle of the Pacific,* and then a half-puzzled look came over her face. 'A conquistador of nowhere,' she shouted through the rain with a smile on her lips.

And then for a moment, she looked at me... After that, she shook her head and got on the radio. Almost instantly, I began to laugh and called over to her. The shore of the island had come into sight.

And, I guess, as I think about it, that's another thing that reminds me of the desert—that type of feeling, that certainty I had on the raft. Because, little by little, after the desert cold had started to set in and the stars were quite bright, I felt like I knew where I was going.

It could have been fatigue from the long flight, the lengthy drive, and the monotony of the camel's loping stroll—it probably was—it was probably just my half-falling asleep that made me stare at the horizon's stars. But then something that, at the time, felt like more than a feeling—no—maybe it was just a feeling. Well, anyway, it was something that had the sensations of a feeling, like a warm pulling in the heart and a tingling in the head. This pulling and tingling—it was... it was... I don't know how else to say it—it was a combined—entwined, maybe—sensation that let me know a certain star would, for lack of an ability to find better words—feel better—

[Several voices begin speaking here all at once—a dozen or so male, two dozen or so female. I can hear several languages distinctly—Mandarin, English, Spanish, Balinese, French, Albanian, and Bosnian, though there are many in the background I can't pick out as easily. Below I've listed individual phrases I caught in the order they appear on the tape with the gender, approximate age, and language of the speaker.]

[Male, 55–59, French]: ... lamp...

[Male, 26–29, Spanish]: ... in the...

[Female, 29–34, Albanian]: ... Absalom...

[Male, 48–50, Mandarin]: ... day of lasting achievement...

[Female, 63–65, Spanish]: ... valley of...

[Female, 70–73, Mandarin]: ... the second labyrinth...

[Sound of feet stamping for six seconds and then radio silence, dead audio for 16 seconds.]

[Female, Tri-Accent]: Did any of the stars you followed become brighter after you followed them, or disappear?

[American]: To the best of my recollection, no.

[...murmuring for twelve seconds...]

[Female, Tri-Accent]: Were any of the stars you followed arranged in any special way?

[American]: I'm not sure what you mean.

[Female, Tri-Accent]: Like this.

[Sound of paper rustling.]

[American]: Yes.

[Female, Tri-Accent]: How many?

[American]: One star I followed toward the end. At first, I thought it was like that—like what you're holding—but as I looked at it, it became just a single star.

[...murmuring for eight seconds...]

[Female, Tri-Accent]: Continue.

[American]: Uh—like I was saying, I would feel this pulling and tingling, but only for an instant, and then I would follow the star I felt the feeling was coming from. Usually, it was a star on the horizon—or one that had just risen over the next dune—but a few times it was one that was already a hand or so high in the heavens. And this continued all night. I half-think of it as sleepwalking through that desert—one dune, after another, after another—till I reached the wasteland beyond. And then I rode over that flat expanse, more or less in a straight line, till dawn's blushing colors covered the horizon—amber, orange, red-gold hues. I remember it like the light we see in dreams—perfect, unflinching, and true.

I rode till the high white heat of late morning broke me and I fell asleep in the saddle.

When I woke, the sun was directly over me. I checked to make sure neither of the two other camels had strayed. Of course, I had leashed them together before I started over the Els, but things happen, especially when you fall asleep: knots lose their grip, camels stop, sit down, or wander. They get stubborn and go back in the direction that they came. You get the idea, but by some miracle, they had moved into single file with my mount as the lead. I checked their roping to be sure it was still fast, and, sure enough, the knotting between the second and the last camel had come completely undone. It was just dragging there in the sand beneath the last camel's jaw.

So, I stopped the caravan, got off, and retied it. When I stood up and looked over the landscape, I saw nothing but the flat line of the horizon in every direction.

Then, when I remounted my camel, I saw it—a large heat shimmer in the distance. I knew exactly what it was and I rode straight toward it. As I rode—as I live and breathe—I swear I saw stars, icebergs, islands, and mists as clear as day in that mirage—I saw, in some form or other, the content of many of my dreams.

And then it, whatever it was, drew nearer and nearer to me, and the closer I got to it, the more I expected that mirror-like haze to fade, but it only shrank—until it was gone and under me and, even then, some aspect—its uneven balance or its exalted light—remained, beneath me, the same.

And then there, half a mile in the distance, was a camp about 50 yards long by 50 yards wide with maybe half a dozen tents of various sizes, the largest of which was maybe eight feet high. Then there were blankets—dozens of them, maybe hundreds, in and around and in-between. The color scheme of the camp was dusty—dull khaki, brown, and gray. But the most striking thing about it, as I approached, was that it looked loose, but was, actually, intricately organized—knitted together, almost, with no more than a few inches between any of its components. Its plotting formed not a square, but a lined, linear—geometrical—shape, like the surface of a circuit board. It was amazing and strange. Strange, too, was that to get this many people with all of that equipment this far out into the desert would have required a considerable amount of effort—camels, trucks, small aircraft—what have you. But there wasn't a camel, truck, or runway to be found. Of course, the sand would cover tracks and bury almost anything, but not everything, and certainly not all visible evidence of any supply chain or infrastructure planning. The more I looked at it, the more it seemed as if it were a puzzle that had arrived fully intact, the pieces invisibly fitted into a flawless and intricate design.

At the edge of this city, my camels came to a halt. I dismounted and walked around the edge. There, lying on the blankets, flat, curled, or on their sides, people slept—I should say lay. I have no idea what they were doing, but I know that on the ground, there, with their eyes closed, they lay.

Their clothes were completely mismatched to the situation. I saw men lying in black and blue business suits, women in sun dresses, children in bathing suits. I saw others, still, in workmen's overalls and soldiers' uniforms and hospital gowns. Each and every one's garments had been faded in the sun, dusted in the sand, and made staunch—starched in the heat.

Every fold in their garments, every weathered blanket or brittle hair of those first moments is etched in my memory because of how strange it all was. And then I smelled it. I knew where I was, already, but then I smelled the saffron on the wind—the blue distorting haze in my mind—rich, full—numbing and alive.

At intervals between the blankets and tents, small fires burned, threading trails of smoke over the landscape.

As I walked among those people, the only sound I heard was the flapping of some of the tent tethers in the wind.

And then I saw, at the far edge of the camp, someone sitting cross-legged on the earth. Since everyone else I saw was sleeping or unconscious, I moved toward the only conscious being in sight. Head down, they sat drawing with a stick in the sand.

As I approached, I saw that their skin was gray, their head was bald, and their fingers very thick and long.

They lifted their head and I could see their face was elderly, their eyes were blue, and their lips were the color of ash. I refrain here from naming their gender because I couldn't see one. Their features could have been described as masculine or feminine, and, aside from their strange color, could have been seen as Asian, African, or Northern European. It was confusing just to look at them, almost like they couldn't be—that they weren't there, except they were.

The 'being'—as I don't know what else to call them—then nodded, as if they were answering the question I hadn't asked.

'It is,' I said, affirming more to myself than to them that where I was, was real, that I was finally standing in the City of Dreams.

They nodded again.

'Who are you?' I asked.

'For what I am there is no name,' they responded in a deep voice.

So, I asked, 'What are you?'

I remember they said, 'A function of time and place.'

I didn't take this as an answer, but being where I was, I didn't really think their answer, in particular, was strange. What was most important was that, unlike everyone else, they were conscious and willing to answer my questions—in whatever way. I had no intention of pushing this being or jeopardizing whatever they might tell me. So, instead of continuing that line of questioning, I asked the only question I had wanted to know since becoming fixated on the idea of the existence of this place.

I asked, 'What is the City of Dreams?'

'For each of them'—the being said and pointed to the camp—'a different dream.'

'What do they dream of?' I asked.

And the being said, 'It is difficult to say.'

At this point, I noticed that the being was not only holding a stick, but making gestures with it in the sand. When I looked down to see what they were doing, I saw something that, if you had told me about it, I never could have believed. I saw that the being had etched a lifelike—and I mean *like life*—replica of the camp's scene in perfect monotone. It made the ritual sand paintings of Tibetan monks—intricate paintings that take an incredible amount of time, patience, skill, and energy—look like children's finger paintings.

It was so perfect that it was almost like the wind's accidental brushing of its edges made it move in a real, even natural way—like the flaps on the tents moved the way they move in real life and the blankets curled at the edges the way they curled where people had lain.

It was mesmerizing. I had a thousand questions I wanted to ask about it—the art, the craft, the technique—but there was only the one I couldn't delay and it was more important than any I had just conceived.

'Could I ask someone what they dream?' I asked.

The being said, 'You may try.'

And then I turned around and looked over the sleeping dozens. I looked over their numbers for several minutes and then moved toward a man only a few feet away. I remember he was wearing a black suit and was sleeping on his side.

I shook him once—and then I shook him again—and then, after rising slightly from the blanket, he opened his eyes. They were obsidian for a moment before they turned gray-brown and then green.

I asked him, 'What are you dreaming?'

I remember the look on his face was one of confusion and he spoke plainly.

'I am dreaming you,' he said. 'Are you not dreaming me?' And then his head touched the blanket once more and he was asleep.

In the same instant I could hear the words the old monk in Kowloon sang in the dark to himself outside his sanctuary, echoing in my mind: 'Are you the dreamer or are you the dream?'

I felt—I felt—I can't describe what I felt. I felt something like displacement, confusion, desperation—like I was somehow in need.

I had no bearings. I had no sense even of what was happening. I had this question and that was it—'Which is it?'—'Which one?' I kept asking myself, 'Which one?'

And then I would ask again—'Which one? ...and then I would ask again—'Which one?'.

I'm sorry... This is difficult for me. If—If you just give me a minute... I'll... Thank you—no, I don't need any water... I'll...

[...radio silence, dead audio for six seconds...]

This whole thing is still very vivid for me...

[...radio silence, dead audio for eight seconds...]

I finally came to my senses and remembered there was someone else I could ask. I stood up to try and regain some of my composure and then I asked the being: 'Which is it?'

The being looked up and stared at me. They said... ... ... They said, 'It is difficult to say.'

Then, as I started to feel sick, as I feel sick now talking about it, they pointed to a place on the horizon. I looked at what they were pointing at and saw a white thing—a dot—then the outline of a van, when I looked back, they were gone—the being, the city, the people—the dream. I was alone.

I vomited—twice—three times.

I was standing in the middle of the road. My camels were gone and the van was coming toward me.

I passed out.

When I woke up, I was in a hospital in Ulaanbaatar. They said that I had almost died of dehydration, exhaustion, and exposure. They said that I was lucky to have made it, that I was lucky to have found the road.

I asked about my camels. They said there were none with me.

I felt better, somehow relieved, like it was okay for it to all have been a dream.

I called Julien and asked about the arrangements for the camels. He said that they had been insured, but that the owners were not happy. I said that I was grateful for his careful planning, and then I almost didn't speak to anyone for three weeks.

I stayed in the hospital for another seven days—my burns were very bad, the opiates they had me on were very good, and I was in and out of consciousness the whole time. It was very confusing. Sometimes I thought it was day when it was night, and sometimes I thought it was night when it was day. On at least one occasion I was looking out one of the hospital windows in my room, and I asked a nurse if she could lower the blinds, as the sun was too bright. She said that it *was* bright—it was bright about six hours ago when the sun was still shining. I mean, I was out of it. I was hallucinating pretty regularly, almost constantly, and, by far, the most interesting part of it, for me, was the conversations I couldn't have been having. I say that because almost everyone I had them with was dead—my grandfather, the milkman we had when I was a boy, J. Robert Oppenheimer, Picasso, Kaiser Wilhelm—you get the idea. The only exception was Bianca. And I say that she was the exception not because I thought she was there, but because she was alive. I knew, even in that state, that she could, in fact, have been there, but since I was more than half out of my mind at the time, I assumed nothing. I just woke up at one point and she was there sitting at the edge of the bed beside me. I smiled at the hallucination and it stroked my arm and kissed my forehead. I laughed and it laughed, then it—well, let me stop. Let me just say that since I have no idea if she was actually there or not, I'll continue by using her name, rather than 'it,' as I wouldn't want to be referred to as an apparition if I was, in fact, there.

So, *she* sat there on the edge of the bed and I recall she talked about a number of things before settling on Andre, the guy she climbed with for six months for that profile, the guy she summited El Capitan with in the dark. She said, and I remember this very vividly, she said, 'Do you remember how I looked at you on the morning he and I got arrested?'

And I said I did, because I did, even then, half out of my mind on oxycodone. I still do—her adrenaline-mad smile, her brown curls sweat-matted against the side of her neck, the calm, infinite cool of her endlessly blue eyes. I do...

'Do you remember what I said to you?' she asked me.

I told her that I did. I said I remembered her telling me something about understanding.

Bianca took my hand and said that was good, that maybe all of what she was about to tell me would make more sense if I kept it in mind. Then she said that what she hadn't told me about spending all that time with Andre on the rocks, in the desert, in the deep valleys, and harsh mountain passes—cold, hot, hungry, and tired—was that he had reminded her of me. Not physically. Andre was a climber, and much taller—and that he spent his whole life somewhere between high and toweringly stoned, but that he was me. Individually, instinctively... maybe spiritually. And that's what she had come to understand. She realized he was going to push toward whatever it was he was after in the same way that I was, and that was something she hadn't seen before. She loved pushing the limit more than most, but not like Andre did, not like me. It was something about watching him bivouacking on all those cliffs and mountains, suspended in a thin, neon-yellow bag over nothing and perfectly comfortable being so. He didn't think about the ground beneath him or the difficulty of the climb before him. He was committed, entrenched and at home. That's what she learned—what made me tick, made me happy, and, well, free. And then, she said, somewhere between the relief of her climb up El Capitan being over and the hot food, warm showers, and clean towels of home, she forgot about it. It never crossed her mind again, until we were in Thailand, in Kamphaeng Phet, when she had that vision of her mother and of what her mother told her. In the vision, she explained, her mother told her about the man Bianca would love in a way she'd never love another. Her mother said things, like that his comfort would be softer than others, that the happiness he brought would be happier than what others could bring—and that those things wouldn't make a garden. At least, that's the way I remember how she said it, and it didn't make any sense to me.

In fact, right then, I was certain I was hallucinating. What the hell could she be talking about? And why did I need to hear it now, laid up in a hospital, half-dead? It—it really didn't make any sense, but she just kept talking, so I kept listening.

She said that her mother was very clear about that last part, the part about the garden. That the man would not make one for her, but that she would be happy when she figured out that the two of them couldn't go any further. Then Bianca said, in a moment of clarity that actually made sense to me, that she didn't understand what her mother had meant. How could a person make her so comfortable and happy, but she couldn't be with him—and what did a garden have to do with it? That I understood. But then, she added that the last thing her mother had said in the vision was that Bianca should, 'Ask the man if he's found what he's looking for.' Then Bianca asked me if I remembered that's exactly what she asked me when I woke up in the room where the shamans had carried us, that room with the gray cinderblock walls.

I told her that I did remember, and then I gripped her hand more firmly. She pulled back slightly and bit her lip. Then I saw that she was starting to cry.

She wasn't crying because she was unhappy, wasn't crying because she was sad, but because her mother was right. Bianca always used to complain about how when she was young, her mother was always right. Not about matters like foreign policy or economic trends, but trivial everyday things. Her mother would guess who was at the door, say it was going to rain when there wasn't a cloud in the sky. That kind of thing. 'Always, always, always right,' I remember Bianca saying, and I remember how mad she'd get whenever she thought about it. So, that didn't surprise me, but I also wasn't sure if that was all she was crying about... Anyway, she made a joke of it—or kind of a joke, in a way. She said something like, even dead—even in a drug-induced shamanic dream, her mother was right. Then Bianca started to laugh. Mentioned that she always hated it when her mother was right, and then she ran two fingers along my neck before she noticed what she was doing and gently pulled away.

Then she said she still didn't know it at the time. And, so, for a while, she forgot about Thailand too. Then, finally, while we were out on the raft in the middle of the Pacific, she knew. Not at first. At first, she said, she was just enjoying how fantastically stupid the whole adventure was. It was insane, she thought, but she loved it... loved me... and loved how much I loved it. And then, as the night went on, she thought about all of it. For whatever reason, she thought about Andre, the shamans, her mother—and that's when I caught her turning it all over in her mind. She said that right when I answered her soft-spoken question, I answered in just the way she thought I would. And then, she said, 'And still, I loved you.' Still, she wanted and needed me. Wanted other things, yes, but nothing she couldn't have with me. Not at that point. And then it began to rain and she got scared and wanted to radio for help. We were lost and both understood how quickly things could go from bad to worse in such deep, open water. So, at that point, she said, she wanted me to comfort her. Wanted me to tell her I had been a fool and say it was time to pull back, to quit testing the edge over which I was sure to one day fall. She wanted me to choose, then and there, our lives over this pointless adventure, over any future pointless adventures. But rather than do that, I pointed at the wild beauty of that oceanic abyss, and she knew. She knew her mother was right, and that I wasn't the man for her. I was a conquistador of nowhere—I'd never lead a less than all-or-nothing life.

After Julien told her where I was, half-dead in a dry, barren corner at the ends of the earth, she felt compelled to see me. Not to tell me why she left years before—we were well past saving—but rather because—[*BEEEEEEEEP*: censored audio of .5 seconds]—she said, 'there are no gardens on your horizon, no lasting rest or happiness. There are only vast stretches of nowhere, always on the verge of somewhere, but never really anywhere'... I remember that very clearly—what she said, the way she said it, the way her eyes were comforting and distant at the same time. And then, she told me that she was happy for me, not in the hospital, but then, on the raft. And not just happy, but thrilled, because she saw how honest and perfect and true I was in that moment on the sea. She said I was full in a way that so few people get to be, and she knew, right then, that it was over. She said something like 'it was a good thing and a terrible thing and nothing anyone could have avoided.'

... Anyway, she said something like that. Or, that's the way I remember it. Or... ... ... My nose—I'm bleeding. Is this supposed—

[...the microphone sounds like it's being muffled for a period of two minutes and ten seconds, the sounds that do come through are soft, as though whispered, but indistinguishable...]

[American]: No, no... So, after that, I really had no idea what has happening. The next time I woke up, Bianca was gone. Not only did I know that I was hallucinating most of the time, but I knew whatever she or that hallucination had said was a pretty good explanation of why we'd ended up where we had. And then that just ran circles in my mind over the next few days... or nights. Whatever it was, whenever I was awake or dreaming or conscious enough in a dream or hallucination to wonder, I wondered about what she said, and I wondered about Andre. If I could have picked anyone else to hallucinate about in that bed, it would have been Andre. Since Bianca—the woman or the hallucination—had said that we were alike, I began to wonder what exactly it was that he was after. I began to wonder what made him keep looking for that 'place between night and day.' Was that what I was after? Did he ever find it? Would I end up unhappy? Did he ever fall?—and that's where my mind always stuck. I would think about that over and over and over again. Did he fall? When he fell, what did he feel? Did he care? And then I would wonder if I were him, would I care? All of this always circling and circling around that one question: What was I after? Otha? The City of Dreams? Bianca's garden? Nowhere?

I—I came to the end of that week in the hospital very shaken, very unsure. Then I spent the next two weeks in a hotel in Ulaanbaatar taking my meals in my room and only going out in the evening for tea.

I thought a long time about the events I just described—both in the desert and in the hospital. I thought very hard about what I knew about my world and what I thought I knew and I decided, in the end, if I wanted to move forward in any way, that I'd never know—that I couldn't know. And after I'd come to that, I started to circle each of the events leading up to that point individually, and, like in the hospital, I became stuck on a single point—though not the same point—this time it was about what had actually happened in the desert. This time, I wasn't hallucinating. I wasn't talking to my grandfather, the milkman, Picasso, Bianca or her apparition. I was thinking—hard and analytically about why I had come out there and the events that had or had not taken place in the desert. I understood that in all likelihood, I had hallucinated—dreamed the whole thing.

But it was so real, even after sobering up from the opiates. That place in the desert—it was as real as you are right now in front of me—every detail—everything I heard, everything I saw, everything I smelled, everything I touched. Bianca in the hospital... maybe, but the desert...

I was reluctant to say anything about what had happened to me there, even to myself, for a very long time. To say that it had been a hallucination, a vision, a dream—anything. How could I know?

How could I know anything if I was the dream?

[...radio silence, dead audio for two minutes and 39 seconds...]

[Sound of metal moving on an unfinished concrete floor that grows louder. Sound of wood moving on an unfinished wooden floor that grows louder. Sound of plastic moving over a finished wooden floor or plastic surface that grows softer. Sound of a wicker object being squeezed or twisted that grows louder. This continues for one minute and 37 seconds before five people speak.]

[Female, 69–71, East German accent]: *Torschlusspanik und vergangenheitsbewaeltigung.*

[Male, 38–42, Japanese accent]: よろしくお願いします...

[Male, 56–58, Peruvian accent]: *¿Aturdir en resol?*

[Female, 44–46, French accent]: *Dépaysement dans l'appel du vide...*

[Male, 51–53, Siberian accent]: бытие.[5]

---

5 This last conversation appears transcribed without translation for several reasons. First, and most simply, each individual phrase is difficult to translate, on its own, into English. Second, when taken as a whole within the broader context of the conversation, each phrase's contextual meaning changes in ways which amount to very difficult, different, and layered individual translations, such that, in all likelihood, the five speakers could be discussing one thing, several things, or one thing and several things simultaneously. Finally, it occurs to me that because of the strange nature of the conversation itself, it could, rather than have any conversational meaning, be a code or linguistic key. The phrases, uttered as they are, could signify identity or initiate some broader context, such as a meeting or event.

Because this has been such a difficult aspect of the project, I've dedicated a large amount of time to it, and, although any translation attempt in a situation such as this is likely to end in failure, I've still worked out several possible frameworks for context and meaning that I've included with the relatively literal translation below:

'The fear of time running out, important opportunities passing and coming to terms with what has been lost.'

'Favorably, of course—with a hope that we can make this work to our advantage…'

'Overwhelmed by the reflection of the sun?'

'A shift of body and mind with the call of the void…'

'Being.'

At first, this may seem like a meaningless arrangement, and, in the event that it is a key, it very likely is in terms of any recognizable, coherent value. Though, when taken only in the context of the content as it appears on the tape itself, the statements do have a type of linguistic momentum.

Perhaps, the first speaker is referring to the fear the American narrator felt in his confusion, perhaps fear that something else will be lost in relationship to that event, either to the American or the broader group making the recording.

Going from there, the second statement could be an optimistic clarification. Specifically, the clarification to turn this or these events in the favor of either the American or the group.

At that point, the third statement reads very differently than it might have. Literally, it makes almost no sense, but if we take the meaning of the first two statements more allegorically, the arrangement is thus:

'Fear of things coming and things past.'

'I hope we can still make this work.'

'When it's shined into the eyes, it can be overwhelming.'

Taken in that way, the third statement builds upon the fear and uncertainty of the first and second and creates a progression of commentary on whatever experience or experiences the group is discussing.

As for the forth, it fits perfectly into that allegorical context, continuing a theme of uncertainty and distress. Of course, the 'void' could be literal or taken figuratively in a number of different ways, in which case the passage reads with more difficultly.

Finally, the fifth either gives us a clue as to the meaning of the conversation or complicates it further. In context, it could be referring to the 'Being' the American mentions or to a state of being, the state that

[End Of Tape II]

---

either the American is in or the state the group is in or one to which they are going. To complicate matters further, this form of the Russian 'being' (бытие) carries with it distinct metaphysical overtones that translate poorly. Because of them, 'being' here could also, or exclusively, refer to life, nature, God, essence, a specific entity, group, or person, the universe, or one's social context. To arrange and re-arrange the translation based on any one of these meanings forms several completely distinct explanations for the text. When each individual phrase is analyzed with such scrutiny, translated with every possible meaning, and applied to the broader context, we soon see an exponential number of possible translations to choose from.

Obviously, this short digression communicates very little, but it does communicate how difficult this passage is to translate and contextualize, and it is with such an understanding that I hope the reader will forgive my inability to properly treat the material.

779J.2314.PPJS
[Tape III]

Date recorded: <u>Approx. 1998</u>
<u>Pure CrO2 coating</u>
<u>AC bias 106.6-128.3 kHz</u>
mostly minimal hysteresis

[American]: After some time had passed, I started to doubt some of my conclusions about my experiences in the Walled City, the Khongoryn Els and Ulaanbaatar, and with some of those doubts came a sort of general questioning of my sanity as well. For maybe about a year after my hospitalization—maybe a year and a half—I was in and out of doctor's offices—psychiatrists, psychologists, counselors—everyone told me the same thing: I had been suffering from extreme dehydration and I was hallucinating. Even when I told them about the swamp, the Walled City, Pofadder—didn't matter. Those were unrelated events. They suggested that the City of Dreams was a symbol. Humans make meaning, they said. Humans dream. Therefore, humans make meaning out of dreams. And, to find several cultures that had all referenced some form of 'the place of dreams' was just a coincidence. There was probably some reference to it in almost every culture, since it was such a basic phrase. We sleep, we dream. It's not hard to infer that we try to come up with a name for that state of being—city, town, garden—*whatever*—of dreams.

That coupled with how obsessed I had become—that I was consistently dreaming of the place—meant that area of my psyche was relatively ripe for any kind of episode or break. The fact that the trigger for my breakdown happened to be that I was severely sun sick in the middle of the Gobi Desert wasn't surprising to anyone in the least.

Of course, I asked if I was psychotic, if I needed to be medi-cated or hospitalized. They said that given the nature of my job and any journalistic need to investigate an odd or strange event, it wasn't unsettling that I had become—how did they put it—'excessively passionate' about the idea of this place. They also said given the obsession—that to some degree comes with the territory—I shouldn't be too concerned. As, in the end, after I was hospitalized and hydrated—that is, after I was done hallucinating—I didn't continue to pursue the fixation. Instead, I questioned my experiences while seeking professional help, and, in most of their opinions, that was, in general, the whole of the matter. They said that questions about one's identity and reality were more and more common later in life and that they were a healthy part of one's existential or spiritual examination of being alive, but that should my need to explore the 'dream' nature of life include jumping off a building or stopping a train with my mind, I should contact them again for more help.

I didn't feel that need, and, in general, I didn't think much about what had happened or not happened in the sun and the heat. I'd had an odd career—many, *many* people could say the same. Hell, Bianca once said she was almost certain she had found Paititi—the Incan city of gold—when an archeologist she was with started to believe an Ayahuasca cult, a cult that also claimed to be werewolves, knew where it was. And Julien once said that he had seen three men turn into two in broad daylight while working with Interpol police who were investigating them for the theft of three Monet's in Venice. Weird is common, in a way.

Then, for a long time, nothing happened that I could consider even remotely strange. Years, actually—almost half a decade, when I think about it. Most of my journalistic work was relatively standard fair—standard for adventure magazines, but not anything exceptionally weird or out of the ordinary.

Of course, a few times, I looked into a haunted house, a bleeding statue, but nothing stood out, nothing rung true. It was all in the name of investigation for a specific commissioned story. The days of working on spec on odd personal interest stories I considered over.

With a focus on paid gigs, I started getting back into a routine. For a while, I got into researching sports and interviewing less-extreme athletes. I wrote a profile of the skateboarder Rodney Mullen, and a piece on the surfer Miki Dora. I don't know if it was a sign of being a little older, having had some adventures, and feeling more able to be at ease, but I stopped, or at least staunched, my extreme adrenaline craving.

I don't mean I stopped doing fun things—I climbed the second highest peaks in both Europe and South America within a year, and hiked, in entirety, the Great Wall of China. But in that same time span, I turned down the opportunity to write a piece about indigenous cannibals in Guam and one about running with the bulls in Pamplona. Both stories seemed needlessly extreme. The police could catch people-eaters and the young and dumb could get speared by bulls in Spain.

I—I guess maybe it was that I was still fascinated by feats of personal limitation—hiking, mountain climbing—but maybe I had lost, to some degree, my intrigue in man versus anything other than landscape.

Competition was something I had come to see as personal, not against something. It was now through pressing against my personal limitations that I thought I could learn more about myself, other people or animals, and my surroundings. In that spirit, I even went on a couple of forgettable arranged blind dates.

Maybe this was something that had come out of—what I saw—as my psychotic existential crisis… maybe.

Anyway, this is a lot of what those years were about for me. And it was pretty uneventful—pretty boring. And then, somewhere along the line, I stopped dreaming.

I don't mean I lost my desire to do or achieve things, I just talked about how I still had goals, but actual dreams—like at night, asleep.

Really, the funny thing is, I didn't even question it. I figured, in some way, that my comfort, my contentment had led to the loss of my nighttime dreams.

No more naked episodes in the grocery store or childhood memories—nothing. Just a black expanse between going to bed at night and waking up in the morning. It felt like anesthesia, if you've ever been under. The immediacy of where you are before sleep, then the immediacy of where you are when you wake up—and nothing, absolutely nothing in between. Really, the most conspicuous thing about it is the gaping maw of its own absence, much like I imagine space beyond the stars or space after everything has pulled itself apart... An endless vacuum without the possibility of coming into contact with anything other than the enormity of its own nothing—its infinite absence.

No content. *Not. One. Bit.*

And—to be honest—it felt *great*.

I focused quite a bit on actually *getting* this sleep. For a few months, even, I only took jobs close to home, because I knew I could get—if I pushed it—eight to ten hours of solid, vacuous sleep.

Eventually, after it had gone on for about a year, I started playing games with it—testing it just to see. I'd watch the most extreme horror films or documentaries about—about, well *atrocities*, and then nothing—no dreams. Then I tried eating different, strange things before bed, because some people have reactions in their sleep to that sort of thing. I'd try combinations, things like sauerkraut, cornmeal, and chocolate syrup. Or I'd try goat's milk, mustard, and chop suey—stuff you wouldn't believe. Anyway, I kept going with it till one night, I woke up and started puking. After that, I stopped, but still, not a single dream.

After another year, I didn't really even think about it and I went about the simple business of living...

'*The simple business of living,*' has a nice ring to it.

Don't you think?

[...radio silence, dead audio for six seconds and then a magnet near another amplifier creating a Barkhausen noise for six seconds...]

Well... Well, anyway, for the most part, that part of my life was simple business and living. I'd even considered settling into an editorial desk job at *National Geographic*. In fact, I was about to put my name in the hat for a shot at the seat, when I had a dream.

In it, a man was sitting at a table before a window in summer, maybe late spring. The light was such that it was either early afternoon or late morning, and the man looked Eastern European, possibly Armenian. The table was round. The man wore a dark gray suit with a dark blue tie, and there was a chessboard on the table—in a position where it was obvious that two players were in the middle of a game.

Mind you, I've never been any good at chess, nor have I ever been particularly interested in it, but I did know that as he moved both the black and white pieces, he was playing both sides.

So—a man sitting before a green window, playing chess with himself—that's it—a simple dream.

I woke up, called the office of the person I needed to talk to about getting hired for the editing job, and, while I was waiting to be connected, got a call on the other line. I hung up on the office and took the other call, as was my habit—always take a bird in hand, that kind of thing.

Funnily enough, it was someone in the same office building calling me. Not the same magazine—but my friend Julien who was now working a sports desk for a different magazine on a different floor in the same building. He said that he had something—not work, per se—but something I might be interested in pursuing.

'All right,' I said, 'what is it?'

He said, 'A chess game.'

I went silent.

'Hello?' he said, making sure I was still on the line.

'Yeah,' I told him, 'I'm still here.'

He asked if I wanted to know more about the game. I said that I was listening, and then he went on to tell me a story about chess engines—that is, computer chess games.

He told me that, until a program named HiTech came out in the late '80s, no chess game was a real match for a real player. Then he told me there were several other programs of note—programs like Gideon 3.1, ChessGenius, Deep Thought, and most recently and famously, Deep Blue, a computer program that had just beat the reigning world champion. He then mentioned that there was another machine, but that this machine was human—a man known as 'The Turk'—a man who could beat, with ease, any living player *and* any known machine.

I asked, 'If this man is so famous, why isn't he the world champion?'

He said, 'That's the thing, that's what's so interesting. He's a living *god* in the right chess circles, but he's not even slightly interested in public play. He just likes the game. And, as no one's professional reputation is ever on the line, everyone seeks him out. Everyone wants to see if they can beat him.'

I asked him if his magazine was doing a story on the man.

He said no, his magazine wasn't doing anything, but he knew where the man's next match was if I was interested.

I asked him if there was a catch.

He said, 'There's no story. And, I don't mean this isn't a great story. I mean, there is no story here. You can go, you can watch, you can probably even interview him, as I'm told he likes to talk, but you can't print anything. The Turk won't allow it. He doesn't want *any fame* or recognition beyond the reputation he already has.'

I asked why anyone hadn't tried to print a story on him anyway.

He said he'd been told by several managing editors that The

Turk had very powerful friends. He said he'd heard a friend of a friend say that a journalist he knew had been asked to withdraw their piece about the man for publication, and that when he refused, he stopped showing up for work. The story goes that he had a secret drinking problem, and that the car accident he had was a result of his even more out-of-control drinking in connection to his girlfriend leaving him. And, because the journalist hadn't given his final okay on the content of the piece after the editors had given their revisions, the piece never ran. It sounds ridiculous to me, it really does, but then again I'm here... and I wonder... Can't help but wonder...

Anyway, given that the nature of the only dream I'd had in half a decade was about a vaguely Middle-Eastern man playing chess—and that it occurred on the night before I received my friend's phone call—I said yes, I was interested in speaking with this man.

He told me that there was a small private tournament once a year where The Turk played most of his games. It was never announced more than three days in advance, but this year he knew it was in a small hotel in Istanbul.

I took his address, thanked him, and then asked if he had seen Bianca. He said, 'Yeah. She actually mentioned that she was going to mail you something. So... keep a look out, I guess.'

It had been years since she and I had spoken, or not spoken, depending on how you look at that time in the hospital outside of Ulaanbaatar. Of course I had written her and called to see if she had actually been there, but I'd never heard back. That's the thing about love—you never know how it's going to go. You never know how people are going to change after something's over, how they're going to take it or what they're going to do. They're not really in your life in the same way anymore... Anyway, for me—for me, I was just excited to get a chance to have contact with someone that meant... that meant what she meant to me. So, in all, it was a pretty good phone call. I thanked him for the message and hung up.

To be honest, I didn't think much about the chess tournament at first. Instead I thought about Bianca for a while, then I took the whole tournament thing as an interesting, but plausible coincidence—remember that it had been a long time since I'd been around anything I'd file under 'truly strange.' I may have also been subconsciously trying to mitigate my own thoughts and feelings about it based on the fact that the last time I had gotten excited about something strange I'd ended up in a hospital, wondering if I was insane.

So, I booked my flight and went about the rest of the day—to be fair, I should say that although I didn't dwell on the trip, I did do some initial research online and then stopped by the library to look into who the 'best' players were in some of the chess journals and magazines, just to be able to recognize faces and names if there really were top players there. It's not that I didn't trust my friend—I did—but it's important to do your own research on *anything* anyone tells you, even if it isn't for a piece. As a journalist, you just can't turn that part of your life off. Then—*after that*, I went about the rest of my day.

The next morning after intentionally staying up all night—reworking and re-working my cover letter for that editing position and hoping to sleep better on the plane—I got on the flight and, to assure my unconsciousness, took a sleeping pill. I was completely out till the flight attendant woke me on the tarmac at Atatürk Airport.

I thanked her for her efforts and took a cab to the old quarter of Istanbul.

I remember the plane trees along several of the boulevards and then, for some reason, really wanting fresh figs.

When I got to the hotel, I asked my driver if there was a market nearby and he said there was one just around the corner to the south. I tipped him well and went inside.

The hotel was small, smelled of cedar, and, except for the several games of chess being played in the lobby, was otherwise completely ordinary.

I knew, at least, that I was in the right place. I also knew that tonight would be the first round of the tournament. I knew this because at the front desk I received a note. Julien had called and left me a message about needing to go to Canada for a few weeks, explicitly apologizing for not being able to be of any more help with my meeting, but also leaving a detailed outline of the next twelve hours—the time in which the tournament took place. He also referred to the games in a cryptic way. The first round—five games—would be played beginning at eight that evening, but he called the games, 'The Five Kings of Spain.' The next three games were to be at midnight, though he called them, 'The Three Rajas of Annapurna.' Finally the last round, one game to be played at four in the morning, was referred to as 'Caesar's Last Collection.' I... I assumed then as I assume now that the desk clerk was just bored and entertaining himself. Nevertheless, it was a simple tournament, if not set to a conventional schedule, and I was almost glad that the whole thing, including its total lack of publicity, seemed completely benign.

I checked out my room—simple, plain, clean—and then I went in search of figs.

When I got just outside the market, I saw a man who looked very much like the man in my dream. I actually considered asking him if he played chess, but I wrote it off as one of those things you think about doing that makes no sense and you never do anyway—you know, like yelling something at a classical concert just because you're not supposed to, or jaywalking in front of a cop. Something stupid, but something you sometimes think about anyway—like a kind of pre-Tourettes thought pattern or something.

Anyway, I found good figs and then I went back to my room. I watched a Turkish soap opera where a man, like I did, checked into a hotel and then went to a market to buy figs. Afterward, he died of a heart attack and his former lover denounced him as a thief and a fiend. It was just a little too much in the direction of that... that surreal type of strange, the uncomfortable type of strange element I had been around before.

Still, I brushed it off—the guy was the illegitimate, but somehow legitimate, heir to a brothel fortune, as well as a blackmailing kidnapper. So, when eight o'clock rolled around, I went down to the small convention room area.

When I got to the large double doors, I saw a standing sign that read *Quiet Please* with a man in a tuxedo standing beside it. I nodded to him and motioned to open the door. He asked for my invitation.

I said I didn't have one.

He then told me that there was no way I could get in, that the event was private and by invitation only.

At this point, I thought this was why Julien had let me in on the event. It was a goose chase to keep me from getting an early audience with the magazine where I was trying to become an editor. The position was high profile and other people would be doing everything they could to keep ahead of their competitors. I figured he must have been working with or working for a different, better friend. I thought that for a moment, and then I remembered it was Julien. The same guy who had gotten me my first climbing interview with a high-profile no-oxygen Everest climber. The same guy who introduced me and Bianca. It was an oversight, a disappointing mistake, and I couldn't even get ahold of him to correct it. Or maybe I just needed to believe it wasn't possible, needed to have somebody in my life who wasn't leading me down a dead end... Maybe, but probably not. The Julien I've known has always been a good man. Anyone who ends up with...

Anyway, I told the man in front of me that I didn't have an

invitation, and he said that he was sorry, but I could not enter the event.

At that moment, the man I had seen outside the market, the one who looked like the man in my dream, appeared behind me and said I was his guest.

The man in the tuxedo held the door open for both of us and we went in.

I said, 'thank you,' and he said, 'of course,' and smiled.

Inside the room, the walls were draped in a lush purple-and-red velvet. The windows were covered, and what could be seen at odd ends behind the draped fabric was old oak wainscoting or the small flashing lights of, what I assumed, were computer servers. In the center of the room were five identical small round tables with five identical chess sets. The room itself was lit by gas-lighting and the whole feeling, despite the computers, was antique.

It was curious and grand, to say the least.

There were 15 or so other men and women in the room, all well dressed. I was wearing a shirt and dark slacks, thinking it would be relatively informal, but I felt very under dressed. Most of the men wore tuxedoes and most of the women wore extremely formal evening wear.

The only other man there whose dress was somewhat relaxed was the 'dream' man who had let me in.

He wore a dark gray sports jacket, a loose white shirt, no tie, and dark pants.

There was some conversation among the more formally dressed members, and then a bell rang.

A few people pulled back two of the curtains and three separate computer towers were revealed. One was obsidian, decked out in LCD screens and large *Do Not Touch* emblems. Another was small, the color and texture of bricks, and had dozens of antennas. The last was, by far, the most impossible, as it was tall, cylindrical, and seemed to be made of water. Well, see-through glass with different kinds of electronic pieces suspended in a mostly colorless, vaguely blue liquid.

A moment was spent with people taking places at the different tables, either as proxies for the computers which they checked with at every move, or as individuals, alone.

At about that point, my eyes had adjusted to the low light, and I could see that, based on the research I had done, my friend's information was correct. There were three Russians I recognized—one of whom was the current world champion—two famous Americans, and one Italian.

Curiously, only one side of the tables had been filled and then a second bell rang.

Each of the people standing at a table played a move for white, and then the man who had helped me to get in walked past each table and made a move for black.

Again, I'm not a big chess guy, but I remember seeing a photo of Bobby Fischer doing something like this when I was young. Even then, I knew by the looks of utter concentration and difficulty on the other men's and women's faces that it was an incredible thing. Now, assuming these three chess programs were as renowned as the human players and on-lookers, which I had no reason to disbelieve, I was amazed.

The Turk, as I now assumed the man to be, was playing effortlessly. Where the other players took time or looked agonized before making a move, The Turk played instantly.

In half an hour, he had won three of the games. After an hour, he had won the remaining two.

Everyone congratulated The Turk and then began to leave. As I had waited a bit behind the others, I approached the man last, and, as I did, he asked, 'You're the journalist, are you not?'

I told him that I was. Then he asked, smiling, if I was going to do a story on him.

Before that moment, I wasn't—and hadn't—been planning anything. I was told that it was a private, off-the-record event, and, ethically, I respected that, but something in me moved, something simple and deep, and I couldn't just watch, so I was honest and said, yes—I would do whatever I could to confirm the event had happened and to get the story out.

I remember he smiled, said, 'Anything for you,' and invited me to dinner in the hotel's restaurant.

I accepted, and then I asked, since it was 'anything for me,' if I could take notes. He said, 'As you like,' and made a careless gesture with his hand. I was almost shocked that he'd accepted my request based on what my friend had told me. I hid my surprise as best as I could and tried to account for why he was speaking to me in such a friendly way. I was told the man was a recluse, not a socialite—and even less, someone who was sympathetic to the attentions of the press. Was it me—had I made some sort of impression on the man—or had my friend lied to me? I didn't have more than a moment to think about it, as I was more than willing to take whatever I could get, but I remember thinking it very strange, almost unsettling. Though after that initial impression, I was too consumed with the prospect of what I might ask at dinner to think about it again.

So, we agreed to meet in ten minutes and I went upstairs to get something to write with and then returned to the restaurant.

When he arrived, he was carrying figs. He said, 'These will be the best of your life.' To be polite, I took one and, in fact, it was the best fig I have ever had, before or since, in my entire life. He motioned for the waiter and we ordered.

I had written in my notes that I had spaghetti Bolognese and that he had a lemon and thyme rainbow trout. I guess that's not really important, but it does let you know the degree to which I wanted notes about our meeting. Ever since having been left high and dry with Otha, I had taken to keeping very detailed notes during interviews.

I remember he tasted three wines, refused two, and had two glasses brought out of the third for himself. He drank slowly, but steadily, and never seemed anything other than completely alert.

After we had settled the circumstances of our surroundings, he told me that I collected odd things.

I didn't really understand, so I said that, actually, I wasn't much of a collector of anything.

He said very precisely, 'This is not true. This is not true at all. You have gone around the world collecting the most odd of odd things—experiences of a fantastic order... in a swamp with an old man, in a desert filled with tents, and in the belly of a fallen city. Tell me, are you chasing your dreams?'

At this point, I had caught on to what he was talking about. The feeling I had in my stomach since eating his fig had intensified, and I now assumed that it wasn't his fig. I assumed it was that the situation had reached beyond the tipping point of what I could rationalize as coincidence and what I would start to call strange.

This man I had never met suggested that he knew about events in my life I hadn't talked about to anyone outside of a professional psychiatric setting or my closest and most loyal group of friends.

Startled, but not necessarily afraid, I told him I had no idea what he could mean.

He asked if I was done playing coy.

I repeated what I had said, emphasizing that I really didn't have any idea about what he could be referring to.

I remember he said, 'True intimacy is having been in someone's dreams. And my friend, I have seen you in your dreams.'

I was speechless, and as unsettled as I was, somehow, I wasn't completely afraid—I was suspended in disbelief, but not completely afraid.

Then he shifted in his seat and asked me if I knew why people called him 'The Turk.'

As confused as I was, I started to try to say something, and then he held up his hand and shook his head.

The people around us, he explained, making a gesture referring to the whole hotel, had given him the name. In one form or another, he told me he had known them for almost as long as he could remember—people who represented other people or knew people that had called him by that name. He said they called him that because they, and everyone like them, thought the type of game he played was, essentially, a game itself. He went on to clarify by saying he was not the first Turk. The first was born a long time before him in the 18th century. He, or it, I should say, as The Turk made clear, was a machine that could play and beat any other player—that *did* play and beat any other player for over a decade. And the fantastic part about it was not that it would win, but that it was what it was—that it was *a machine*—a machine before computers *or electricity*. Back then, that was its whole appeal—the sheer impossibility of its existence, and, of course, that impossibility, with time, came to be seen as proof of a devil's hex—proof that it was a cursed, unnatural apparatus beyond man's scope or understanding. People saw it that way because it beat monarchs and peasants and skilled chess masters alike without pause, doubt, or mercy. But, at base—it was a deception executed with quick wits and cunning. It was a magic trick, a hoax, where an accomplished player would hide inside the machine's bowels and operate it without ever giving himself away.

And, although it lost a few games in its operation over the course of half a century, no one, except its owners and operators, knew its secrets—no one suspected anything.

Now, The Turk wasn't suggesting that the people around us thought he was a machine. Obviously, they could see he was a man, but all of them—every single one—he assured me, thought he was a fake, a liar, and a cheat. They all thought he was so good that he had to be hiding something from them, something that, if they knew it, they could use against him and then be unbeatable themselves.

It was at this point that he started to laugh. I thought, naturally, he might be disappointed or even angry, but the man just sat there and laughed. Then he spent a moment smiling to himself and sipped at his wine. I can still see that smile, bright as a Sunday morning in May—careless or carefree. I still wonder... Was it careless or carefree?

Anyway, he went on by saying that it absolutely wasn't true. That he knew I was thinking he had to be withholding something from me—which I was thinking. Then he said it was much simpler—that, no matter how it seemed, it was only misunderstanding. His being in my dreams, his playing the way he played—all of it—everything, he explained, was ordinary. He said, 'There is no secret. I am just an odd thing like all of the other odd things you have seen.'

The man smiled and the food arrived.

I don't remember what anything I ate tasted like, but I remember that I ate all of it, in silence, and with haste.

At the end of my meal and the height of my confusion, I asked: 'What do you believe is an odd thing?' And although I was relatively inarticulate, being that I was only repeating what he had said, the basic meaning of what I was after—that I wanted to know what he meant, about himself and the other experiences I'd had, what they 'were,' so to speak—came across clearly.

He said it was a good question, a question worth pondering, but that he knew I had asked another question—a similar question, but not the same—on another of my crusades. And that, like that time, this was a labyrinth of a problem, impossible to precisely explain. But, he said he would be willing to guide me as best as he could through the corridors toward a vague understanding—as long as I was willing to proceed.

I was hesitant, as I was nervous about the unreality of the

situation. I hadn't forgotten the... complicated nature of my previous experiences, nor had I been able to forget their intrigue. I say that, not because I wasn't able to return to my daily life— I already told you how I had just done that for some time, but— as evidenced by my inability to ignore this tournament—my interest in the truly strange never completely went away.

Now, as before, I was being promised half-answers, half-mysteries. This man, The Turk, was himself mysterious. I'd heard of yogis who could hear thoughts and enter dreams, but I had never met one. Of course, I'd investigated three or four in the past, and their methods, though fascinating, never seemed more than suggestive—nothing more than obvious to anyone who knew anything about subliminal stimuli. For instance, one guy I investigated claimed to make people fall asleep on command, but, because he kept saying he could do so to his audience, and then reinforced the thought with suggestive cues, like yawning or slightly closing his eyes or relaxing his posture, people bought it whole cloth and passed out on the ground, in chairs, standing. One guy he put to sleep swore that it was the only way he could get good sleep. He said that he suffered from horrible night-mares whenever he slept away from the 'yogi.' The nightmares he described would always start out in a house or car or boat by a beach, and then he would find a door in the sand. When he opened the door, he found what he described as a velvet feel-ing, obsidian chasm. He said that the chasm itself was alive, felt like the soft shock from a low-level electric charge and moved like breath clouding over a cold windshield. It sounded terri-fying, and it was fascinating, but completely unreal. The snake oil salesman that put him to sleep always made sure to talk to the man about certain subjects before he put the guy out. The subjects were always related to kind and gentle events intended to comfort the man. I picked that up immediately. But this man, The Turk, on the other hand, hadn't been given anything. He wasn't telling me about anything vaguely—he was telling me about my experiences and dreams—and he was doing so with great detail and accuracy.

As I felt clear-headed and in command of my senses, I felt sharp enough to keep up in general with where this chess genius was going, given I had been around and had some experience with other strange happenings, I accepted his offer.

He seemed pleased, ordered more wine, and offered me some. I refused again. Then he proceeded to ask me a series of questions.

The long and the short of it was something along these lines:

Why did I feel compelled to pursue these fantastic experiences? He told me he understood why they'd interest me, but why is it that I obsessed over them, pursued them so unreservedly?

I said something like… I'm a journalist, and it's my duty to learn about and explore the world, to follow the stories through to their ends. He then asked what I wanted to learn. I said something about the human condition, the nature of people—something grand and vague like that, anyway. Then he asked what I had learned. I didn't even know where to start, or how to respond, so I told him that of course, I had learned many things. He shrugged off my dismissal, telling me that I had an entire collection of first-hand experiences that were of value—from chasing sham stories of bleeding statues and haunted houses to the truly remarkable like the events in the Gobi desert—that had to have imparted some impression on me. What was it I had learned? I said something as vague as my first answer, something like that people are all the same—that they all want and need the same things. Again, he asked more specifically what they needed. I said, sarcastically, that all men need food and water. Yes, he conceded, this was true, but I didn't learn that in any of my travels to distant lands. No, he pressed further, what he wanted to know was what I had learned about all men from all of my searching all over the world.

At this point, I stopped answering his questions dismissively and thought about the answer. I thought about all the humanitarian answers—did all men need love? Many men I had met claimed they didn't want or need anything like it—like the monks or adrenaline junkies. I thought about purpose, but several I had met only wanted to wander deliberately, aimlessly—dreamers and lotus-eater types. Then I thought about good will—many didn't believe in the concept or hadn't experienced any such thing—like some businessmen and many politicians I had met. Then I thought about countless other things, and there wasn't any one I could think of that all mankind needed. One group needed one thing, another group needed another, and so on and so forth for everything that I came across or considered at the time.

And then, I saw him smile as if I were answering a riddle.

I couldn't think of anything. So I said, 'No, not really.'

'Good,' I remember he said. 'Then you know this place—the whole world—is a strange place.'

At that moment, he looked at his watch and said it was time for the second round. I looked at my watch and, in fact, it was midnight.

I followed him once more into the conference hall and watched much of the same thing I had observed before, except this time, I couldn't stop thinking about why it was so effortless for him.

Yes, he had said he was an 'odd thing,' that there was no explanation for how he did what he did, but that couldn't stop me from trying to explain it—to understand it in some way.

So, I watched and I watched and I watched. This move, that gesture, that turn, that maneuver. Everything he did I watched carefully—trying to find something that I had been told was impossible to find—that even if I knew what to look for—that is, even if I understood the game of chess to a great degree— I couldn't find.

The only consolation I had in the task was that it kept me

from thinking about what had just happened, about how intimately this man seemed to know me.

I didn't miss a single indifferent glance.

It was effortless—maddeningly effortless in the same casual, completely matter-of-fact way in which he had spoken to me.

And then it was over. He had beaten two exceptionally difficult computer programs and the world champion in less than two hours—all under the influence of more than six glasses of wine.

When it was over, he smiled at me and asked if I'd join him for coffee and a walk. As upsetting as the situation was for me—and, differently so for the others in the room—I felt compelled in my own way to play the situation out, to go along with whatever was happening.

So, as soon as we were sipping café au lait back in the hotel's restaurant, I tried a different approach. I tried getting at him through his secrecy. I thought perhaps it was only the way in which he did the things he did that gave him his mystique, his unreality—the sudden tournament, the moniker of 'The Turk,' the all-night play—I thought that maybe if I took away some of his personal mystery, it would be easier to better see what I was missing—whatever explained as ordinary the extraordinary impossibility of the situation I was in.

I told him that in the interest of the article I was writing, it would be useful to have more than just his stage name. 'The Turk' was compelling as an alias, but readers would refuse any story about a man without his real name, his history—who taught him how to play.

He said his name was Ahmet Akdari. That he had been born in Sofia, Bulgaria, to a poor, uninteresting family. His father had been a stonemason and his mother had been a seamstress. He said he was born an insomniac and had been one all his life. With so many hours at such a young age, he looked for ways to occupy his time. First, by exploring his home and then, in turn, the city around him. When he was four, he began doing the laundry, going to market, and cooking simple meals for his family. At five, he left home and started working as a bus boy in a local café. At six, a drunk asked him how many games he had seen played in the small restaurant, and he had replied by sitting down across from the man and moving a piece. The drunk, two professional gamblers, and a priest lost every game they played that night. By the time he was seven, he was still undefeated and had moved on to exploring different parts of the city in the long hours when others were dreaming. He said in that time, in particular, when the city was asleep, the farthest corners and most secluded reaches of its landscape opened to him and he saw and took part in strange—unbelievable—things.

I asked him about that landscape, about what strange, unbelievable events he had been a part of and seen.

He smiled at me and then looked off into a distance that seemed far beyond the walls of the hotel. Then he said that he had met Time in person, plotted a treaty with Death, and held Infinity between the first and middle finger of his left hand. The last thing he said—the bit about Infinity—he said while holding up the two fingers of his left hand.

We drank our coffee and, quite simply, I believed him. I had assumed he would be unwilling to tell me anything, and when it turned out to not at all be that way, I felt completely disarmed. Obviously, I didn't understand what he could have meant when he talked about Time and Death and Infinity, but I believed— I still believe—that I couldn't. The man was too plain, too amazing to follow into a world where he could know me and my experiences so thoroughly, a world where the capable and possible were limitless. The man, if nothing else, was completely genuine. In many ways alarming, but very genuine all the same.

After a moment, he asked if I had discovered in his response what I wanted to know, if that had helped answer my question about my strange experiences.

I said, no, that I was as completely lost as when I had asked the question—in truth, probably more so.

He smiled and asked if we might start our walk.

I agreed and we walked toward the lobby doors. At that point, I didn't know how—no matter what I said or tried to say—I could get at what I wanted to know. So, I just asked him why, exactly, he couldn't explain what he considered an 'oddity.'

He moved his head to one side and—when I think about it now—I can still see the concerned look come across his face. He stopped, opened the door for me, and I stepped outside. I noticed it was very cold for summer in Istanbul—and then, I noticed, without alarm, that where I just was in Istanbul was a very, *very* long way away.

I say that I was without alarm because, without explanation, I was—really. In retrospect, I suspect that the transition was so sudden and strange, and the environment was so still and quiet that for a few moments, I felt nothing... except a kind of... a kind of quiet inside.

I remember there was snow on the ground, the dark shadows of mountains in the distance, cloud cover and stout wooden buildings with thatched roofs all around. I recognized the buildings—they were a type of mountain cabin found in a few villages in northern Japan, in the Gifu Prefecture—the kind with steep, sloping angles and weathered frames.

Then, beside me, as calm as he had been during any of his chess games, The Turk looked up at the clouds. He exhaled the smoke-like condensation from his lungs and spoke quietly, almost to himself.

He said, and I will always remember, 'I have asked myself that question an infinite number of times. How does one explain what is incapable of being explained?' Then he said, almost as an afterthought, 'It is beautiful though, is it not?'

I nodded, still lost in what I can only think of as a form of shock I had never experienced before. He then motioned for me to follow him as he turned back.

I saw him walk through the unlit doorway of a cabin behind us and then disappear. I followed and, *not* to my surprise, I was back in the hotel lobby.

The Turk said that it was time for another game, and I followed him, bewildered, into the conference hall.

This is where things fell apart for me. I started running over things again and again in my mind.

I thought about what he had insinuated at dinner—that he'd been in my dreams and read my mind. I thought about how he beat the most brilliant giants of the chess world with obvious— impossible—ease; how he, presumably, had just transported me halfway around the world and back in a few short moments; and how, unavoidably, recounting these things to myself—as the feeling of shock faded and the obvious, threatening, and terrifying reality of the situation set in—I began to seem, in my own mind, to be crazy. Or, I thought, if I wasn't yet crazy, I soon would be as there was nothing to explain any of the things that had happened to me in *any* way.

And that's where I was for the rest of The Turk's final chess game. He stood calmly placing pieces neatly on a chessboard five feet from me, and I couldn't decide if I was already crazy, would soon become crazy, or was too crazy to tell what type of crazy I was or was becoming.

When he had won effortlessly, again, he thanked the players and the programmers for coming and hoped that he might have the honor of playing some of them again at the next tournament.

I sat in the same position as they filed out of the room around me, and, when it was just the two of us, The Turk sat down across from me.

He sat for a long time in the plush leather-backed chair

opposite me in that dark purple and velvet room. And then, after a while, he spoke to me.

He said, 'And now, we are in the labyrinth where we have been, except you can see it more clearly.'

I had no idea what he meant or could mean. From my perspective, I was more lost than I had ever been, and I didn't see anything more clearly. I just sat there—trying to make sense of anything.

He told me I wasn't crazy. At least, he explained; not more or less so than anyone else that had ever lived.

And still, I said nothing.

Then he said that was the problem with bizarre experiences.

At that moment, the ceiling lit up, and I looked up, thinking a light had been turned on.

Instead, what I saw was a clear night sky—perfect and bright—in more detail than I could remember ever having seen it. It was so clear that, for a moment, I forgot I was probably hallucinating.

And then I returned to my thoughts, their concern and their weight.

The Turk went on by saying that was the problem. That odd things were so odd that they poked holes in our worlds like stars piercing the night sky. Unexplainable, we try to explain them and, when we can't, we become very afraid. He said he could see that I was obviously very afraid, and he would help me make sense of the evening's events by telling me what I was most afraid of. Then he snapped his fingers, shook his head, and did a 180. He doubled back and said that, because I was so afraid, he couldn't tell me, he could only tell me when I wasn't so afraid. In order to do this, in order to tell me what the thing was that I was most terrified of, he said he'd put it behind a door in my dreams. And that, if I became adventurous again, I could find it there—*there*—in my dreams...

I can still see him clearly. Sitting calmly, making no sense at all and smiling under those stars. The way he smiled was in a half-sad, half-affectionate—mocking kind of way, like he wanted to feel for me, but he couldn't under the circumstances. It was both endearing and estranging.

After that, he stood up, paused as if he was trying to remember something, and then left. As one foot passed through the doorway at the end of the room, the stars vanished with the lights and I was left alone in the dark.[6]

Of course, I packed as quickly as I could and got on the first plane. When I landed in New York, I admitted myself to a psychiatric hospital in Manhattan where I then spent the next two weeks certain I'd be staying there for the rest of my life. It was large and on the 18th floor of a building with views of Central Park. I reviewed the strange, scattered events of the last decade with every doctor there, and everyone told me the same thing—diagnosis was not a snap decision. It could be several things. Some allergic reaction could have caused my confusion in the swamp. Dehydration and sun sickness could have caused the hallucinations in the desert. And as for the tournament in Istanbul, it could be a simple stress-related psychotic break. Obviously, fixation played a part in all of it—I was, and had to admit to myself in that place that I was more than fascinated, but *fixated* on the strange. And then there was my fear, the anxiety that all of this had caused in my nervous system. That, in itself, they said, could be some form of PTSD. When taken as a whole, the three events together could be seen as something like brief reactive psychosis—where the patient is psychotic for brief periods separated by long stretches of time—or it could, potentially, be a case of late-onset schizophrenia.

---

6   Here, concurrently with the narrator speaking for 17 seconds, I hear whispering in something like a liturgical Latin; however, the consonants seem to be pronounced in a more Germanic fashion. The only words I'm sure I hear are *in the blue garden* though I can't make out any more than that.

Really, they said, the key was to wait.

As I wasn't violent with myself or others, and as I was otherwise unconfused as time went on about the nature of reality outside these events, they said that, in all likelihood, I wouldn't even need medication, except maybe for my anxiety.

They were alarmingly good doctors. I say that because they were so cautious and careful with their diagnosis, so at ease—really—that it unsettled me. They weren't calling me crazy, which in some ways made me feel better, but in others made me feel worse—I wanted the stability of reality, even if the reality was upsetting.

But life, as everyone knows, isn't black and white, but shades and shades and infinite shades of gray. I remember telling a Doctor Susie Dreyfus in the hospital that—as the Turk had said—a door appeared in each of my dreams ever since the night we met. The doctor nodded in the affirmative as I imagine she does hundreds of times daily to hundreds of different patients, and said that it didn't surprise her at all, that it wasn't even necessarily unhealthy. She said that the unconscious was a difficult thing, that it often worked as the mind's way to unravel stressful situations. So, to see what I saw wasn't necessarily suggestion at work, and certainly not some surreal reality, but just a stress response. I remember the look on her face was one of unconcern. 'It's funny,' she said, 'but life is strange like that... Dreams are odd things.' I felt shivers down my spine at those words, but I knew she said what she said without any intention.

It was with her that I would talk about the details of my experiences while looking at the small trees in the park surrounded by the huge walls of that concrete jungle.

I remember I asked her, 'What does one do if they're crazy?'

And, for whatever reason, she said, 'What does one do if they're not?'

The hell of it is, I couldn't answer. I couldn't answer that question. My life hadn't been lived in a way where I had any idea what normal people did. I only knew that I wasn't one of them. Instead of even trying to answer it, I asked what she would do if she was crazy, and she said, 'I'd focus on treatment, simple things and simple pleasures.' Then I asked what she'd do if she wasn't crazy, and, because she felt I wasn't crazy or that everyone was crazy, she said, 'I don't know, but I'll be sure to let you know if I'm ever in that situation.'

Maybe it was just humor, but I didn't laughed. I think she took that as me not liking her joke, but really, it was just like almost everything else I'd wanted to know about, everything over the last so many years of my life. I'd ask a question or go after an answer, and someone would throw me headfirst into a paradox. My life—my entire life was a living, breathing paradox. I was just afloat in an ocean of ambiguity, and not even a doctor—a sworn health professional—would throw me a life preserver. Yeah, I guess I didn't see it as funny... She and the rest of them were so casual, so certain my existence was normal—was right as rain.

I waited in the hospital for two weeks to pass, and when it had, they recommended that I keep in touch with a doctor back home, but that I was otherwise stable and sane.

And that's how things went, again, for quite some time. I ended up taking a different editing job and I all but stopped going out on assignments. Instead, I did what all people do when they're not doing one thing—I did some other things. I started fly fishing to relax and I got into gardening and woodworking to help with the anxiety.

Around that time, that's when I got Bianca's letter. Really, it wasn't a letter at all. It was just an invitation—a wedding invitation, actually. I was invited to Bianca's wedding—Bianca and Julien's... Yeah... Well... Yeah... It's hard to talk about, but not in the way you might think. It's hard to talk about because I couldn't figure out how I felt about it for the longest time. I say that because when I read the invitation, I didn't feel anything. Intellectually, it made sense. They were journalists. I hadn't really settled down. Julien was taking easier and easier gigs, and they'd known each other from way back. In a way, I was happy for them—really—but that doesn't mean I thought that I should feel happy. So I thought about it some more. Shouldn't I have felt upset? Shouldn't I have felt betrayed? Yeah, I think so—but that's just it. I was thinking about it. I wasn't *feeling* anything. After a while, I figured that I got what I needed. Closure, that type of thing. They were together, I was alone. They had each other, I had the opportunity to chase after anything I wanted. The more I thought about it, the more it made sense. In a way, she had her answers. She trusted her experience in the jungle. She believed things about gardens, and happiness and comfort. She knew I was like Andre. She knew I didn't have any of those answers. She knew he and I both wouldn't stop until we found or tried to find what we were looking for—or died in the process. And maybe that's the best thing that came out of our relationship. Because, more often than not, when I think about her, I find myself wondering if he fell or if he made it. Did he find that place? Did it kill him?

I guess it[7] could have been repression, denial, or shock. But as the months passed and the date of the wedding approached, I just smiled whenever I thought about it. I really felt happy that they had found what they were looking for... so few of us make it that far... And since I felt like I had what I needed from the whole thing—when the day came, I didn't go. They had their garden, as Bianca had wanted—and I had mine. Granted, mine was more literal, but they were both quiet lives, and I wasn't interested in re-tilling old soil. So, I watched the dill, carrots, and

---

7 Here, concurrently with the narrator speaking for half a second, an object bumps the microphone and a minimal amount of feedback is created. I include this note as the words *I guess it* in the transcription are my interpretation of what I hear the narrator saying, though he may, in fact, have said something different.

tomatoes come up and built a root cellar for the fall. Life was simple, plain even. I had gotten to a point where everything was almost completely non-strange. Everything, except for the door in my dreams.

And so it was. No matter what I dreamt about—my mother holding my hand as a child, climbing Ausangate in the Andes, tending goats on an Irish farm in the middle of a long winter—the door would always be in the dream. Right there—obviously—and it was always the same. It was made of a weathered, unfinished oak, splintering at the edges with a dark iron door-knob. It would be beside my mother's closet, on the ledge in the middle of the mountain, or standing in the middle of a grazing field—no matter the dream, the door was always the same.

And, whenever I saw it, I knew exactly what it was, what it meant and what I didn't want to see.

This went on for years—four years I think, actually, and then I decided something had to change.

Instead of trying to fall back into the dream after having seen the door, as I had been trying to do for years, I just stood in front of its frame, examined its edges, felt its surfaces—anything and everything till I would wake, and then I'd go about my day.[8]

Of course, I spoke with my therapist about the development, as I wasn't looking—again—to go insane, and they said they thought it was a healthy exploration: That I knew it was just an aspect of my unconscious and that to deal with the fear and anxiety surrounding it was a good and necessary thing.

They encouraged me to explore my fears around my experience of reality. I told them I had done enough of that for one lifetime.

---

8   Here, concurrently with the narrator speaking for one second, I hear a male voice whispering in an English accent a single word: *Aramec*. After some research, I discovered that this could be a romanized version of the name Arcturus, the fourth brightest star in the night sky.

But, as time went on and as I continued to explore, inspect, and contemplate the dream, I knew that deconstructing my fear was the only option, even if I wasn't ready to walk through that door.

So, I turned to research on the little I knew about the dream, or rather, the little I knew that had to do with the dream.

Ever since the beginning, even in the swamp, everything had been about understanding in a certain, specific way—a way that I eventually picked up on in the Walled City.

I began to study, as best as I could follow, Zen dialogue, the complexities of Hindu philosophy, the Greek philosophers' discussions on paradox and other difficult problems and impossible things. And then I sat with this research and became less and less afraid. I became more comfortable in my ability to see that these ways of thinking were deliberate exercises in futility. That they, in fact, were nothing to be afraid of because they were just words and ideas rather than concrete, real things.

And then, after some time, I was less afraid. So much so, that one night while asleep, I walked to the door in my dreams, turned the handle, and stepped inside.

I half-expected to just see a mirror image of myself on the other side. It made the most sense that fear was just fear of one's self—that type of thing—but it was The Turk, sitting at a wooden table in a room with no windows and no ceiling, just a clear overhead view of a bright blue sky.

He motioned me to sit in the chair opposite him, and I obliged.

'Are you ready?' he said.

I hesitated, thought about it, and finally said, 'Yes, I think so.'

'The thing you are most afraid of,' he said in his thick Eastern European accent, 'is that there may be more and less to this world than there seems to be.' He went on by saying that this world—this whole world—could be as strange and wonderful and fantastic and unknowable as this dream or any other.

That all of this—everything—is an odd thing beyond explanation entirely.

With that, he rapped his knuckles on the table and laughed quietly to himself.

He told me that he could see me thinking as plainly as when I was what I would call awake. Then he asked me how I would explain what was happening—how I would explain any dream. Then he said I would explain it very simply. I went here—did this—this and that happened—and then I'd wake up. Which, is true. That's exactly how I'd explain it, except he pushed the question further. He asked, what would happen next? And I thought, obviously, I'd go about my day, but he just smiled and said, 'Exactly. Your day?' he asked. 'What is that?' And then I got it. I'd get up—do this and that—such and such would happen, and—all of it—from the moment I woke up *or, from the other side*, from the moment I went to sleep, it was exactly the same thing—the same motions, the same routine. Then, whether he said it first or I thought it—or I thought it and he said it at the same time, the two questions that seemed like one felt overwhelming in my mind, 'Which one is awake? Which one is a dream?' Each one tore at my mind like two ends of a chasm opening onto an infinite void. I couldn't—absolutely couldn't—decide. When I thought of where I was, sitting in what I thought was a dream, and how almost the same type of thoughts and same impossibilities had happened in the swamp, the desert, and the hotel—a place that I thought was awake—I couldn't think, I couldn't feel—I don't know how to communicate it, but for lack of a better way to say it, I—I couldn't *be*. If both were the fiction of a dream, I was unreal. If both were fact—with all of the fantastic and astonishing events I had taken part in, had seen—then I was equally as incapable of understanding myself or my context, as no concept of real I had ever known had included any such absurdity. I sank and I sank and I sank into that chasm, and when I realized where I was or where I thought I was, I yo-yoed between blacking out and experiencing everything as some kind of hyper-full, hyper-alive. The blacking out felt like a type of fracturing where the experience of the dream bled together— colors, sounds, sensations—into a kind of fabric, a fabric that was woven of that place's essence, its reality—the fabric of a dream. And then that fabric, built of a restructured unreality, folded in upon itself in a type of geometry I've never seen, like a piece of paper that shimmered every color, sound and sensation were pushed and pulled in all directions and then, suddenly, removed itself. Removed itself in a way that… like how the wind just stops or the moon disappears behind a group of clouds. Sort of like that, except total and complete. Now when I say that, I think of a total and complete absence, a nothing, but that thought is an image of a blank, black expanse. And this—this was the removal of that background, the deconstruction and elimination of even absence. That was the peak of that blacking out. Now, the hyper-full, hyper-alive feeling was one where, instead of fading away, the fabric of the dream got louder, grew larger and overtook me. I—I don't have any real way of describing that experience, but an idea of a description comes to mind—a kind of metaphor. It's like if this room we're in, and everything beyond it composed an endless ocean, and we were tied to a mast on a ship that faced a wave—a wave that drew the endlessness of that ocean into itself and plummeted upon us as we sailed into it—and as it hit us, we took it in, all of it—the sublime totality of reality ripping us apart and beyond anything we could have… anything beyond… any anything… something like… No—no. It's no use. Even in a description, it falls apart. But that's some of the idea of what it was like.

This went on—this yo-yoing between inconceivable extremes—for some… some something. I'd say time, but because I consider what happened to have taken place in a space that could not be defined as anything like a sequence of events, I only have… I only have words that might point in the general

direction of what I mean. I guess—maybe—if you could lo
at all of time and then step outside of it, that's where I was—
maybe before or after... At any rate, when I came out of wher-
ever I was, I was still in that open-roofed room with The Turk,
and I eventually made out that he had been saying something,
over and over, for some time. At first, I could only make out the
first part: 'Can you see? Can you see? Can you see?' And then,
after a while, I got the rest. 'Can you see... that everything is an
odd thing?'

And I did. I understood, for the first time, how I could never,
ever understand—how it was impossible, actually, to explain
how any part of life could be seen as more than an unexplainable dream—how the events of being awake proceeded and
were as strange and marvelous as any of the miracles that occur
when we are asleep. The strange situations I found myself in
and events that I had seen—in the swamp, in the desert, in the
hotel—were just that—the wonders of dream. It didn't matter
if I was awake or asleep, the ones performing the impossibilities
seemed to understand the same—the how and why for them,
for me, for everyone would always remain unexplained. Their
way of life was as mysterious to themselves as it was for you and
me—it was just what was happening for them, the same as the
sun rising or setting in a day is what happens for us. Probably
for them, I think, it was just a bit more of a lucid dream. And
what's more—I felt completely plain. No fear. No anxiety. Just
the simple recognition of an impossible state of affairs.

And then I had something I hadn't had since before I met
Otha. I had a question that I wanted to ask out of innocent
curiosity—a curiosity free from needing an answer—a question
for the question's sake.

I asked, 'If this and everything else is as you say, what is
behind the dream?'

I remember The Turk smiled at me and said, 'That is a good
question.'

I woke, and that was the end of the whole thing.

I have looked for the door many times, both in the hours I have been awake and in the hours I have spent in dreams, but I have not found it since.

I didn't feel the need to tell a therapist or anyone else what had happened. It was never relevant in any situation, until now, when you asked.

Does that answer your question?

Now—

[Sound of a bell ringing for six minutes and 37 seconds in the note of D.]

[American]: It sounds like a similar thing, the way they describe it. Cold, like slipping into a bathtub filled with ice in a dark room. Your body starts to slow and you can't move much. Then the walls start to move like water, like clouds... almost—

[End Of Tape III]

Afterword

In the decade that has passed since the tapes found their way to Amrapali Singh's office, this manuscript has only been seen by about a dozen people: Amrapali, my former employer, myself, and a handful of publishers.

It was given to me by my former employer, ███████████, on July 23, 2006. In the interim between my sophomore and junior year of undergraduate study, I worked as her office assistant in Cedar Rapids, Iowa. As an English major looking to enter the publishing field, I was grateful for the opportunity to work for a summer as an intern for such a well-respected freelance editor. The job was simple and ineffectual. I took out the trash, cleaned the office, picked up meals, walked her dogs, and took calls and messages. I was compensated with experience, an opportunity to read manuscripts, and a small stipend.

Mostly, I read cookbooks, biographies, and technical manuals. Occasionally, I read fiction. My instructions were to forward anything that looked close to being publishable. I seldom forwarded anything in my first two months with her. That I recall, I forwarded a cookbook composed of recipes from Mandalay restaurants, a technical manual on a piece of accounting software, and a technical manual on an open source programming environment. None of these books were published. Though ███████████ had three readers, one was off for the summer, and she was skeptical about my talent for picking good manuscripts, and rightfully so. The three that I passed on to her were unpublishable. Two others that I had deemed unpublishable, she sold within a week on the recommendation of her other reader.

The manuscript that you've just read, I rejected, as I thought it was undeveloped, inconsistent, and insufficiently detailed. My co-worker forwarded ████████████ the manuscript with a note for exactly the same reasons, except they thought of the project as fiction and considered it publishable under the corrected genre.

I then received the manuscript a second time from ████████████ and was told to do some fact checking. I called the office of Amrapali Singh, PhD., and spoke with the campus operator about her office hours. I had called while she was still away and was asked to call back in two days. When I called back, I was told that no such person had ever worked for the University of Dutch Harbor. Of course, this was disconcerting, but I assumed it was a mistake. I called back three more times over the next week and spoke to two department heads and a professor. No one knew who I was talking about. I figured that either my information was incorrect or that I was being put on for some reason. I read Amrapali's cover letter a second time and researched the conference where she had supposedly met my employer in 2004. Sure enough, when I called the organizers of the conference, they assured me that Amrapali was an annual speaker, that she did, in fact, work for the University of Dutch Harbor and that she would be returning to Phoenix for the conference at the end of September.

From there, I e-mailed her associate, Claude D. Montclair, PhD., at the University of Northwestern Paris, using the name of my employer, as her office instructions were to use her name in order to assure all e-mails received proper attention. I immediately received an automatic reply from his e-mail address informing me that he would be out of the country for six days. When I e-mailed him a second time six days later, my e-mail was returned undeliverable.

When I told ███████████ about what I had found, she thought it funny. She laughed and shook her head. I assumed she figured the manuscript was a dead end when she pointed at it and said I could learn a lot about publishing from a manuscript like this. She then picked it up, put it in my hands, and told me to find a publisher for it. I read the look on her face to be malicious, but I took the instruction as a challenge nonetheless.

Two weeks later, ███████████ did not show up for work on time. Just before lunch that day, a gentleman in a blue blazer who identified himself as Augustus Stephens said that ███████████ had been brought into ███████████████████. I knew she had worked as an independent contractor for them [that publishing house] for many years. I also knew their contracts were not only prestigious but lucrative. That she would leave her own employment for such an offer was plausible, but that she would do so without telling her two employees seemed unlikely. Mr. Stephens said that she had asked him to close her affairs in Cedar Rapids. I made no objection.

I cleared out my desk, added the manuscript to a box of my personal effects, and left with a severance check totaling more than I had been paid all summer.

To say that it was unusual would be an understatement. To say that I felt safe in the presence of Mr. Stephens would be a lie.

As the summer was almost over, the timing was excellent, though, needless to say, I felt unresolved. I went back to school at the end of August and then, with some of the money from my severance, I attended the conference in Phoenix.

I was now very curious about the manuscript, and all of my experiences with ███████████ and the atmosphere she created around publishing made me insecure about my candidacy for employment in the industry. She had challenged me to get the manuscript published, which made me feel invested in its outcome. I imagined that if I were able to get it published, with it being such singular material, that I might land myself a job in New York or Chicago. It was a perfect storm for attending an obscure conference on sound and books in Phoenix that fall.

After I arrived, I saw that the events with Amrapali Singh had been cancelled. In their place were comparable panel discussions covered by other professionals. When I asked the hosts about her absence, they told me she had been offered a job in Chiang Mai and that she'd informed them she wouldn't be able to attend that year.

That's when it began for me. Coincidence is one thing, conspiracy another. I returned to school and went back to my studies. I also made copies of the manuscript and stored them in various locations, mostly safety deposit boxes and rent-a-lockers. Once I had ensured that several copies existed, I began to research the different names in the book. I did this knowing full well that someone might be watching me, so I went about it inconspicuously. I used pay phones to make inquiries at truck stops and gas stations when I traveled by car out of town. I did the same with internet cafés and libraries, and then I began to think that there was too much of a pattern. All of the inquiries were mostly within the same state, so I began to travel farther just to do research.

Needless to say, I told no one what I was doing, except when I pitched the project to publishers. And, although I found very little, I almost always found some evidence that indicated I was chasing real people and events. To be sure, I'm no detective, and only—at best—an amateur at any of the investigative arts, though I was surprised to see how far simple curiosity took me, and in what small ways my life became like that of the journalist on the recordings.

To list what I didn't find would be more exhausting than what I did. So, to that end, I will list what I've found in relationship to the names and events described in this manuscript.

There is a record of a Bianca Terrazas and a Julien Belmonte leasing an apartment outside of Paris in 1999. I tracked this down after reading the only published article I could find by Mr. Belmonte. It was an op-ed in a French culture magazine on Parisian homelessness and its growing underground youth culture. In it, he mentioned that he and his partner had moved into one of the old quarters of the city in order to investigate the situation. Fortunately, I was able to find public records dating back to their time in the area and, eventually, contacted the owner of the building they had lived in. This was costly knowledge, as I discovered Mr. Belmonte's article by way of the internet on a dead site that's copyright was last updated in February of 2001. That, in itself, was free, but getting a copy of that magazine took a lot of time and money. I had to bid on lots of old French magazines on eBay for almost a year before one came with the issue I needed. Then, I had to pay a French student from the Deep River Community College in Blue Hill, Nebraska, to speak to the landlord, as I don't speak French or any of the other languages listed in the manuscript, except English.

The next breakthrough I had was in 2008, when I found a used copy of a self-published book for sale on the internet, whose description mentioned an Andre Esquibel, a Basque climber matching some of the characteristics of the Andre in the manuscript. When I received the book, I discovered it was an ex-library copy from an industrial city in Vietnam. The pages which mentioned Andre were missing, as well as the index. Only a third of the book remained intact.

As for Ms. Singh, I did find a copy of *The Sound of Time*. I found it in a used bookstore in Phoenix about six miles from the convention center where the annual 'Sound in Written Texts' conference is held. It's a scholarly and well-documented publication with interesting conclusions. In the back, a person matching the exact description of Ms. Singh is accompanied by a picture of a stately woman that looks to be in her sixties or seventies. I've never encountered another of her books for sale online or seen mention of her anywhere since. The new organizers of the conference say they've never heard of Ms. Singh.

The narrator's name is mentioned only once and redacted, but based on his descriptions of the incidents upon which he had reported, I've concluded that he could have been one of the following three people after cross-referencing hundreds of internet and private database searches for articles containing those topics:

Jude Henderson: a correspondent for several nature magazines and websites from 1978 to 1998. Found dead in a bar in western Sudan, 2002.

Alexander Ray Williams: a correspondent for several nature magazines and websites specializing in extreme sports and human interest pieces. He was also the one-time editor of *The Odd Adventure Internet Zine*, which ceased to circulate after July of 1998. Found dead in Akron, Ohio, of a heart attack from complications associated with diabetes in 2000.

Charles John Holt: a prominent freelancer for *National Geographic*, *The Smithsonian*, and *Audubon Magazine* up until March of 1998. Declared dead in absentia in December of 2007.

Of the three, I lean toward Mr. Holt; however, it's important to note that I've included all of them as possible candidates because none of these men had any surviving family members. This was important in my investigation, as when I researched a specific individual, any inconsistencies were usually clarified by a family member.

Also, it's important to note that I am here assuming the narrator is dead. They may be alive, but if they were, it's likely their name would still be in circulation.

I have found no mention of any other name or address in the manuscript, including Marilyn Eldritch—the audio expert Amrapali sent the other copy of the technical readouts of her analysis to, or the Biblioteca Nacional de Investigación de Buenos Aires.

For a time, I considered publishing the manuscript on a personal blog, a website, or on some other mass media internet platform. I did, however, change my mind. As there is almost nothing on the internet that makes mention of any of the individuals connected with the manuscript, I decided against this course of action. I believe there to be a strong probability that any such mentions may have been altered or erased.

I have chosen to hide the names of my former employer and the publishing house associated with her disappearance not to hide information from you, the reader, but to protect my former employer, her other employees, and their associates, should they still be safe. My intention is to have no one come to any harm.

As it may concern the reader that the true author of this work is Amrapali Singh, and not myself, N.J. Campbell, it is important for me to explain the reasons this work has been published under my name as a fictional account. Although several publishers were interested in this manuscript initially, they refused to publish it on the grounds that it was, firstly, not my work and, secondly, insupportable as a non-fiction account. I have gone with the current publisher because they have agreed to let me assert in this afterward that the account is, in fact, non-fiction, even if, for legal reasons, it must be published as fiction. The way we have worked around the issue of copyright is that I and the publisher have agreed to hold all proceeds in a trust for Ms. Singh, should she step forward for them, for a period of seven years. After which, if no such claim is made, the money will then be transferred to a trust designed to further investigations into the curious uncertainties presented in this account. The publisher and I feel that in any event, ultimately, Ms. Singh would have wanted the material to be published, and that, as an audio research historian fascinated with the origin and circumstances surrounding the creation of the tapes and their anomalies, she would desire and approve of any effort to find them and further their investigation.

Finally, as of this day, the 19th of March, 2017, I do not know what happened to any of the people connected with this manuscript. I do not know if they are alive or dead. I do not know if they or I have been watched or ignored. I do know that the milestone of having finally gotten this manuscript into the hands of the public is now complete. What began as a challenge, as I mentioned in the foreword, eventually turned into a crusade, and I have taken it as far as I, personally, can, but I know it can go further. Even if this publication is eventually discovered, the copies individually traced, collected, and burned, one other person may have read the story. One other person may ask: where have these people gone? What do the tapes mean? Who is the Biblioteca Nacional de Investigación de Buenos Aires?

N.J. Campbell
Fairfield, Iowa
March 19, 2017

ACKNOWLEDGEMENTS

A book is the result of a lifetime of experiences. If any given experience were added or subtracted from the whole, then it would invariably change the nature of the book. Perhaps the change would be small and imperceptible, such as a slightly different word choice in one or two passages, or, perhaps, the change would be substantial, leading the book to become a novella of fifty pages or a more sizable novel of five-hundred. It's difficult to say. But regardless of what it would be, it would be due, in part, to each of those experiences and each of the people that participated in or facilitated them in whatever way.

So, I would like to start by thanking everyone who participated in or facilitated any of my experiences, in whatever way, leading up to the publication of this book. Without you, this book would not exist—or, at least, it would not exist in its current form. I owe you all a great deal of gratitude.

More specifically, I'd like to thank my mother and father, Craig and Abigail; my brothers, Sam and Carl; my grandparents; my aunts and uncles; cousins; other extended family members; friends; teachers; professors; mentors; editors; and those who work for my publisher, Two Dollar Radio.

I'd also like to lavish praise on several individuals whose contribution was particularly significant to this book: my friend Brian Stains for his early editorial support and friendship; Eric Boyd for his tireless encouragement and good council; Joey Del Re, Joseph Mayfield, Surya Gied, and Angelo Wulf for their continued artistic inspiration and friendship; John & Carol Longhenry for their scholastic reverence and the impression it made on me at a formative age; Grandpa Charlie for editing my first book at the age of ten and for reading with me as a small child; Nynke Passi for critiquing and enduring my prose as a college student; Eric Obenauf for taking a risk on an unknown author and for his patience and kindness in discussing and refining the book with me; Eliza Wood-Obenauf & Haley Cowans for their copy edits and style guide support; and, finally, Hannah Foster for her kindness, support, tenderness, and companionship.

Two Dollar Radio
Books too loud to Ignore

ALSO AVAILABLE Here are some other titles you might want to dig into.

THE ONLY ONES NOVEL BY **CAROLA DIBBELL**

→ **Best Books 2015:** *Washington Post*; *O, The Oprah Magazine*; NPR

← "Breathtaking." —NPR

INEZ WANDERS A POST-PANDEMIC world immune to disease. Her life is altered when a grief-stricken mother that hired her to provide genetic material backs out, leaving Inez with the product: a baby girl.

SEEING PEOPLE OFF NOVEL BY **JANA BEŇOVÁ**

→ **Winner of the European Union Prize for Literature**

← "A fascinating novel. Fans of inward-looking post-modernists like Clarice Lispector will find much to admire." —NPR

A KALEIDOSCOPIC, POETIC, AND DARKLY FUNNY portrait of a young couple navigating post-socialist Slovakia.

THE REACTIVE NOVEL BY **MASANDE NTSHANGA**

← "Often teems with a beauty that seems to carry on in front of its glue-huffing wasters despite themselves." —*Slate*

A CLEAR-EYED, COMPASSIONATE ACCOUNT of a young HIV+ man grappling with the sudden death of his brother in South Africa.

THE GLOAMING NOVEL BY **MELANIE FINN**

→ *New York Times* **Notable Book of 2016**

← "Deeply satisfying." —*New York Times Book Review*

AFTER AN ACCIDENT LEAVES her estranged in a Swiss town, Pilgrim Jones absconds to east Africa, settling in a Tanzanian outpost where she can't shake the unsettling feeling that she's being followed.

SOME RECOMMENDED LOCATIONS FOR READING TWO DOLLAR RADIO BOOKS:
On a beach, in the dark, using a lighter's flame; While getting a tattoo of an ex-lover's name removed; While painting the toe nails of someone you love; Or, pretty much anywhere because books are portable and the perfect technology!

Two Dollar Radio
Books too loud to Ignore

ALSO AVAILABLE Here are some other titles you might want to dig into.

SQUARE WAVE NOVEL BY **MARK DE SILVA**

← "Compelling and horrifying." —*Chicago Tribune*

A GRAND NOVEL OF ideas and compelling crime mystery, about security states past and present, weather modification science, micro-tonal music, and imperial influences.

HOW TO GET INTO THE TWIN PALMS
NOVEL BY **KAROLINA WACLAWIAK**

← "Reinvents the immigration story." —*New York Times Book Review*

ANYA IS A YOUNG WOMAN living in a Russian neighborhood in L.A., torn between her parents' Polish heritage and trying to assimilate in the U.S. She decides instead to try and assimilate in her Russian community, embodied by the nightclub, the Twin Palms.

MIRA CORPORA NOVEL BY **JEFF JACKSON**

→ *Los Angeles Times* **Book Prize Finalist**

← "A piercing howl of a book." —*Slate*

A COMING OF AGE story for people who hate coming of age stories, featuring a colony of outcast children, teenage oracles, amusement parks haunted by gibbons, and mysterious cassette tapes.

SIRENS MEMOIR BY **JOSHUA MOHR**

← "Raw-edged and whippet-thin... A featherweight boxer that packs a punch." —*Los Angeles Times*

WITH VULNERABILITY, GRIT, AND HARD-WON HUMOR, acclaimed novelist Joshua Mohr returns with his first book-length work of non-fiction, a raw and big-hearted chronicle of substance abuse, relapse, and family compassion.

Thank you for supporting independent culture!
Feel good about yourself.

Books to read!

Now available at **TWODOLLARRADIO.com** or your favorite bookseller.

THE ORANGE EATS CREEPS
NOVEL BY GRACE KRILANOVICH

→ **National Book Foundation '5 Under 35' Award**

← "Breathless, scary, and like nothing I've ever read." —NPR

A RUNAWAY SEARCHES FOR her disappeared foster sister along the "Highway That Eats People" haunted by a serial killer named Dactyl.

NOT DARK YET NOVEL BY BERIT ELLINGSEN

← "Fascinating, surreal, gorgeously written."
—*BuzzFeed*

ON THE VERGE OF a self-inflicted apocalypse, a former military sniper is enlisted by a former lover for an eco-terrorist action that threatens the quiet life he built for himself in the mountains.

THE VINE THAT ATE THE SOUTH
NOVEL BY J.D. WILKES

← "Undeniably one of the smartest, most original Southern Gothic novels to come along in years." —NPR

WITH THE ENERGY AND UNIQUE VISION that established him as a celebrated musician, Wilkes here is an accomplished storyteller on a Homeric voyage that strikes at the heart of American mythology.

THE DROP EDGE OF YONDER
NOVEL BY RUDOLPH WURLITZER

← "One of the most interesting voices in American fiction."
—*Rolling Stone*

WURLITZER'S FIRST NOVEL in nearly 25 years is an epic adventure that explores the truth and temptations of the American myth, revealing one of America's most transcendant writers at the top of his form.

Did high school English ruin you? Do you like movies that make you cry? Are you looking for a strong female voice? Zombies? We've got you covered with the Two Dollar Radio Flowchart. By answering a series of questions, find your new favorite book today! → TWODOLLARRADIO.COM/PAGES/FLOWCHART